TO CATCH
A
COWGIRL

TO CATCH
A
COWGIRL

•

Suzanne Walter

AVALON BOOKS
NEW YORK

Wal

PRINTED IN THE UNITED STATES OF AMERICA
ON ACID-FREE PAPER
BY HADDON CRAFTSMEN, BLOOMSBURG, PENNSYLVANIA

To Sue Fickel, Sharon May and Ann Peach for guiding me on
this journey.
To my parents, Fred and Vera,
for believing in me even when they thought I was losing my
mind.
To my family and friends who have supported me,
and my editors Mira and Anees for buying my manuscript.
And finally, to Nosey, not only do you live on in my heart, but
within the pages of this book.
Love ya, baby.

Prologue

Oklahoma
One year earlier

Martina Lewis found him nearly naked at the Hide-Away Motel. Heartache threatened to steal away her words, but she pressed past it. "Roy Sullivan, you are a low-down, two-timing, lying dog!"

She couldn't believe she had become a rodeo cliché. Another cowboy's girlfriend who sat at home while he did the circuit . . . and all the buckle bunnies too. She tried to push past Roy but he wouldn't let her into the room. "Alison! I know you're in there!"

"Now baby—" Roy began.

"You said you wanted me to be a sweet little housewife when we got married," Marni gasped as she tried to pull him out of the way. "But you really wanted me to give up barrel racing so you could horse around the rodeo circuit!"

"Now baby, this isn't as bad as it looks," Roy pleaded.

1

"I'm not stupid, you know. I saw Alison's red pickup parked beside yours."

"Be reasonable, Sweetie. That could be anyone's truck."

Marni stopped grappling with him and put her hands on her hips. "It says *Barrel Bunny* on the bug shield, Roy. How many trucks have you seen like that?"

"Marni." Roy reached for her. "Honey. We can work this out."

She pulled back. Her skin crawled at the thought of touching him after what he had done.

"I don't think so, Roy."

They'd worked it out once before, but then it had been only a rumor. This time the proof was right in front of her. She'd been a fool in the past; it wouldn't happen again.

"Why did I ever give up barrel racing for you?"

"If you really want to do this barrel thing, we can talk."

"You know what? I'm going to do 'the barrel thing' . . . without you. The engagement's off."

The last time Marni saw Roy was in her rearview mirror. His awkward shuffle as he tried to hold his pants up and chase her car as it peeled out of the parking lot was an image she burned into her memory so she'd never make the mistake of hooking up with a cowboy again.

Chapter One

"Easy, Twister," Marni soothed the big gelding. "Wait for it."

She chewed on her bottom lip and kept an anxious eye on the ring crew. They were just about done reassembling the barrel course after the tractor had dragged the arena to make it ready for the next five competitors. This part always took forever. Marni hated being the first in after a drag. The wait for the tractor and ring crew was agonizing—and gave her too much time to think about what could go wrong.

The smell of livestock and the noise from spectators clashed with the heat and dust, swelling from the ground in hazy waves over the rodeo arena. Butterflies rippled in Marni's stomach as she anticipated her barrel run. Nervousness made her clench and release the reins. She could feel Twister's muscles bunch as he tensed underneath her and knew he was eager to be released.

Focus, Marni. Keep your mind on what you have to do. She watched as the last rodeo hand cleared the ring. The

3

whistle sounded to indicate the course was ready. She took a deep breath.

"Now!"

Twister exploded from the chute and blasted towards the first barrel. Time slowed for her as they charged into the arena. It was hard to believe it would all be over in seconds.

The crowd and the noise of the rodeo disappeared as her world narrowed to the course in front of her. They galloped toward the first barrel. Marni sat deep in her saddle and cued the gelding with her voice.

"Whoa!"

Twister set up underneath her, his hind legs bunched as he slowed, collected, and carried himself around the can.

"Let's go, Twister!" she barked and pulled herself forward on the saddle by the horn.

He charged at the next barrel. Marni could feel him gather and push off, each stride eating up several feet of ground. She sat back again.

"Whoa!" she urged.

They set up for the second can and raced around it. As they went past, Twister slipped and scrambled to regain his footing. They brushed the barrel, but luck was with them and it stood back up, saving her a five-second penalty.

Twister streaked at top speed across the arena toward the final can.

"Whoa!"

Adrenaline pumped through Marni as she hissed at Twister, "Get outta here, Boy!"

She leaned forward in the saddle. Horse and rider shot toward the narrow exit chute, their hearts beating a thunderous staccato. Marni heard the timer beep as it shut off. They flew out of the arena at full speed into the empty alleyway. She slowed Twister and strained to hear the time over his pounding hooves.

The announcer's voice crackled over the loudspeaker, ". . . and a time of 15.213 seconds for Marni Lewis and Lookout Twister! That moves them up into second place."

Marni released the breath she'd been holding. She leaned over and gave her gelding a hug and a few pats. Her hands shook as she sat back up in the saddle. She took a deep steadying breath and released some of her pent-up excitement as she exhaled. "Good Boy, Twister. Next time we'll take first."

Twister snorted and huffed in response. He pranced sideways as Marni dismounted and rubbed his head against her shoulder once she was on the ground. "Enough!" She giggled. "I promise to brush you down as soon as we get to the horse trailer."

"Marni?!? Since when did they start allowing men to run in the barrel racing competition?" Jake asked Larry, the burly circuit blacksmith.

Larry laughed. "Harrison, you've been away too long. Her name's Marni and she's no man. She's one of the new up-and-coming barrel racers on the scene. Pretty good too."

Jake strained to look over the crowd and caught a glimpse of the tiny woman who led away a lanky bay quarter horse. She stopped and bent over to tighten her bootlace. When a spectator passed in front of him, Jake raised up on tiptoe to maintain his view. A familiar old desire ignited inside of him.

Wow! That is one fine-looking lady. Wonder if she would let me get close enough to get a better look?

"Tell me more," he said to his stocky companion.

"Well for starters, she ain't fer you," Larry drawled

around the horseshoe nails he had just put in the side of his mouth.

"And what's that supposed to mean?" Jake was a bit annoyed. Yes, he had had a reputation in the past, but goodness knew the last year and a half he lived like an old bull put out to pasture. Actually, his good-time cowboy routine had ended long before that. Before he moved back from Dallas, before he bought his parents' ranch . . .

Before Carol-Anne. She had taken his pride and half his life savings with her when she left. He grunted at the memory.

Larry ignored Jake as he picked up Bart's hoof and arranged the horseshoe on it. "Marni's been on the circuit for almost a year and I ain't never once seen her give any cowboy a chance."

The hammer clanged as he drove in the first nail.

"Not that they haven't tried neither."

CLANG.

"Those bull riders have been tripping all over themselves trying to impress her—"

CLANG.

"—along with the bronc riders and the steer wrestlers. She just ain't interested."

CLANG.

"Guess she knows better than hitching up with a cowboy."

CLANG.

"Wish I were a little younger. I'd show her how a good woman should be treated."

"Then you're saying she's—"

CLANG.

"Not for you. Yup, that's exactly what I'm saying." Larry chuckled and put down Bart's hoof.

Jake glared.

"From what I've heard she came out of a bad relationship. 'Stead of running away with the circus, she joined the rodeo."

"Same thing, isn't it?"

Larry snorted and turned back to Jake's gelding. "Tell me about it. Can't help but feel I'm surrounded by clowns." Larry gave Jake a significant look over his shoulder. "So what made you come back, Harrison? Thought you were through with this business. Ya didn't say anything about coming back to the circuit last time I was at your farm."

"I'm here to sell my horses. I have to demonstrate they can perform around cattle. I have the right stock, but I can't sell them if I don't show them off. Figured this is as good a place as any. Besides, the rodeo's in my blood like a disease. I could never completely give it up."

"You sound like the rest of 'em. Not a lick of sense." Larry finished filing the last hoof on the gelding. "Here ya go, Boy, good as new." He turned toward Jake and spit the unused horseshoe nails onto his palm. "Next time think about getting 'im done before you come to the rodeo."

"Next time come out to the ranch when I ask and you won't have to do a rush job on him here," Jake goaded. Larry was like every other good blacksmith in Texas, hard to find and never available when you needed him. He was as difficult to corner as a rogue cow.

"Darn smart-mouthed cowboys. No respect, no money, and not the sense God gave 'em!"

"Nice to see you too, Larry. I'll pay you when I get my prize-winner check."

"Yeah, yeah. Where've I heard that line of bull before?"

Jake started to lead Bart back to his truck before Larry could slip in another comment. He decided to take the scenic route around the rodeo ring. More specifically, past Marni and her horse trailer. He just had to see if she was as good-looking close up as she appeared to be from a distance.

He rounded the south side of the arena and caught a glimpse of Marni as she walked away from the wash-up area with one very wet horse in tow. Curly auburn locks danced down her forehead and into her eyes. He had the urge to brush them away for her and feel their silky texture. Her hips swayed gently as she walked away from him and he was pleased to catch another glimpse of her amazing legs. All in all she was an even better sight up close.

Jake thought it was as good a time as any to introduce himself, so he hauled Bart over to her rig. Her horse was tied by the hay net and she had just disappeared into the front of the trailer when he got there. He prepared his best pick-up line and put on a cocky grin before he swung open the dressing room door.

"Kate, would you close the door? I'm not putting on a show here," Marni said, looking down as she unfastened the last button on her shirt.

Jake's greeting froze in his throat. He wanted to shut the door . . . knew he should and walk away before she caught him.

She gasped and yanked her shirt closed.

He reluctantly looked up into a pair of very angry brown eyes. "I—"

"You—you—pervert!" Marni ground out between clenched teeth. "Just what do you think you're doing? Are you some sort of Peeping Tom?" She gripped her blouse in front of her.

Jake winced. "I—"

"You what? What possible reason could you have for

barging into my dressing room and gawking at me like a possum in the headlights?"

Think, Harrison, think! She said something about a Kate. You know a Kate! "I was looking for Kate," he blurted out. "I didn't know you were changing in here and when I saw . . . well, you know . . . I forgot what I was doing." That didn't even begin to explain it.

"Have you ever heard of knocking?" she demanded.

Darn! Still mad! "I am so sorry, Ma'am, I forgot my manners. Maybe if you do up your shirt we could try this again?" *What am I saying?*

"Get out!" she shrieked, turning red. She wrenched the door toward her and slammed it shut in his face.

Jake stumbled back into his forgotten horse. "Good first impression, Harrison," he griped. "She won't forget you any time soon." He turned Bart back toward his horse trailer to tack him up.

As he tied his gelding to a steel frame, the barrel racing results crackled over the loudspeaker, reminding him of the reason he was here in the first place. He rushed to saddle Bart for the start of the calf-roping class and tried to forget his encounter with Marni Lewis. Adrenaline kicked up in his veins and he wasn't sure if it was the cowgirl or anticipation for his class.

He waited for the calf to be released. The gate clanged open and it ran out into the rodeo arena. Bart broke out of the chute behind it and Jake threw his lasso. The rope unfurled in the air and landed over the calf's neck and shoulders. Bart slid to a quick halt and the line jerked tight, stopping the calf. Jake swung out of his saddle and ran toward it.

Visualize your goal, he reminded himself. Suddenly he pictured Marni, cowboy hat pulled low, a beckoning smile on her lips. For a moment he forgot where he was as he became lost in his fantasy. The calf swerved toward him and he got knocked over by his rope. His imaginary Marni laughed at him.

"Darn it, Harrison!" he scolded under his breath. "Concentrate on what you're doing."

His cheeks burned as he untangled himself, wasting precious seconds. He threw the calf to the ground and got his pigging string tied around three of its ankles without any more problems. He threw up his hands to signal he was finished. With a soft curse, he ambled back to his horse.

Beneath the brim of his Stetson, he spied his buddies as they snickered at him from the rail. But it was the watchful gaze of a certain barrel racer that sent a prickling sensation up his neck while he waited in the sun.

Jake swung back up into his saddle and squirmed. Sweat trickled down his back and beaded on his forehead. Was it the heat, or her? It irritated him that she had witnessed his blunder.

A whistle shrilled through the air and broke his concentration. At least his calf stayed tied, even if his time wasn't any good. But there wouldn't be a prize check for him today. After the ring crew released the animal, he coiled up his lariat and pigging string. He urged his chestnut gelding out of the ring. He could still feel Marni watching him and knew she was the reason he'd screwed up his ride. If he'd kept his mind on the calf roping instead of her, he would have avoided the rope when the calf had swung at him.

"A little rusty aren't you, Harrison?"

From Bart's back, Jake glared down into the steady blue eyes of his nemesis, Sonny Reid, the sheriff of Meridian. They had had a long-standing rivalry. It started over a bicycle when they were seven, and escalated to include girls, trucks, and horses.

"Maybe you're getting too old to play this game," Sonny prodded. His tongue was a silver hit with the ladies, but it had never once been used to charm Jake. It wasn't only his charm the women liked; Sonny had hair the color of a bale of straw and eyes the shade of a cold Texas sky.

Irritated, Jake slapped his rope against his leg; he shouldn't let the sheriff goad him, but he did. "Your old man doesn't seem to think so. He's coming by the farm to pick up the horse he bought from me tonight."

"It takes more than nice stock to make a good calf roper."

"I know. Still having trouble getting a rope around those calves?" Jake couldn't resist the barb. It was petty and childish, but then so was the rivalry between them.

The other cowboy's back stiffened, "Well, Jake, I'm still beating you."

"So you are. Enjoy it, because I'll be catching up soon." Jake turned his horse and headed back to his truck. It'd be a cold day before he'd let Sonny get the better of him.

Jake dismounted at the trailer, took off Bart's saddle, and swung it into the bed of his truck. He laid the damp saddle blanket on the hood and led Bart over to the hose to be rinsed off. The cold spray hit his horse and he smiled as the gelding snorted and danced under the cool water. He got as much of a shower as the horse, but what the heck, he figured he needed it.

Cold droplets sluiced down his face and splattered against his chest, chilling his overheated thoughts. That would teach him to lust after women while he roped calves. "From now on we'll keep our minds on training and selling horses, right, boy?" he said to his soggy gelding. In response, Bart shook water all over Jake.

"Let me guess, you're trying to tell me I'm all wet."

Marni watched for the cowboy-pervert as she returned to the horse trailer from the entry booth. She'd been surprised when he had burst in on her, but more so by the sudden craving she'd felt for him. The desire she saw ignite in his eyes reminded her it had been a long time since she had had a boyfriend.

But Roy had swept her away and then left her with only broken dreams. No man would do that to her again, especially not some sorry excuse for a Peeping Tom.

A smile escaped her as she fingered her check. Dad would be proud. She'd finished third overall and gained enough points to put her in second place for the year-end awards. Of course it was still early in the season, but she didn't plan to lose that championship buckle because she hadn't tried hard enough. Maybe she'd call her dad when she got home. He worried about her if she didn't check in with him at least once a week.

Kate and Ben, Marni's friends, had brought her to the rodeo. They weren't parked far from the hose where the horses were watered and washed off. She suspected they had picked the spot so they wouldn't have to carry the buckets so far. It also positioned them in an area where all the rodeo participants eventually had to come; the perfect social place.

As Marni approached, her gaze was drawn to the washing area and the rugged cowboy who had brought his horse over for a hose-down. It was him! She blushed all over again. She tried to glare but instead slowed down to admire the view.

Finest-looking darn pervert I ever laid eyes on.

It was like a sequence from a dream, and she found she couldn't pull her eyes away. The sun sparkled through the water as it rained down over the horse. Some of it splashed up onto him. One drop slid down his forehead over the bridge of his nose and fell off to cascade past his full lips to his chiseled chin. From there it rolled down his neck, past his Adam's apple, and pooled with other droplets at his throat before sliding beneath his shirt where only Marni's imagination could follow it. She looked back up, remembering the vivid blue of his eyes and his long black lashes. Dark brown hair peeked out from under his straw cowboy hat and curled on his damp neck. Marni felt unwanted desire unfurl in her stomach like a trail of smoke.

"His name's Jake Harrison." Kate strode up behind her.

Marni jumped, startled at being caught. She flushed as she turned to face her hauling partner. "You know him?" She tried not to sound too surprised, but she'd thought the guy had made up that line about looking for Kate.

"Sure," the other woman replied. "Jake's been involved with the circuit since he was a kid. He's been away from it for a while, but now he's back again."

"Just what are you two gossiping about and is it anything good?" Kate's husband, Ben, was a big, stocky man who towered over his wife. They made an odd couple since Kate was petite, like Marni. Married young, they shared a common interest in horses that kept them together through the tough times.

"Nothing to worry your pretty little head about, Honey," Kate purred.

"With you two, I always worry." Ben's expression turned serious. "I hope it had something to do with barrel racing. From what I saw out there you could both use some work."

"You should be pickin' on those big old steers instead

of harassing these two beautiful women, Ben," Marni heard the stranger say. He walked up, tugging his horse behind him. A prickling sensation rolled down her spine and she wondered how he could stir a response from her after their embarrassing first encounter.

"Well, I'll be! If it ain't Jake Harrison. What brought you out to play, Boy?" Ben cuffed the other man on the shoulder.

The gesture almost set the stranger off his balance, but he recovered. "Apparently I'm here to make a big fool of myself and give my horse some exercise."

Marni snorted and Jake eyed her warily. Maybe she was being too hard on him. She honestly doubted he had opened the trailer door on purpose. He had seemed more shocked than she had been.

"So why are you really here?" Kate asked.

"I'm trying to show off some of my new stock. Good thing they perform better than I do."

"Is this the four-year-old you bought off of Kevin Brewster?" Ben asked.

"Yeah, he's six now," the cowboy replied somewhat absently as he caught Marni's eye. "I liked him so much I bought the stud too. . . ." His voice drifted off.

That seemed to be Kate's cue. "So Jake, have you met our friend Marni? She keeps her horse at our place and is renting one of our bunk houses for herself."

Jake ripped his gaze from Marni's. "What was that, Kate?"

Every time he looked at Marni, it was like he was drawing her into a world where it was just the two of them. It was unlike any feeling she had ever experienced before.

Kate smirked, then repeated the introduction.

He stuck out his hand and smiled. "Pleased to meet you, Darlin'."

There was no doubt about it, this guy was slick. Marni definitely couldn't trust him. He would lure her in the way Roy had. She took his hand and was gratified by the look of anticipation in his eyes. His grasp was warm and firm. It sent unwelcome shivers of awareness up her spine.

Okay, so you're attracted to him. It doesn't mean anything. Besides, he's a pervert; don't forget how he ogled you in that horse trailer. There are lots of other handsome guys around and I bet none of them *are perverts.*

But none of them affected her like he did either. As he released her from his grasp, he slid his roughened fingers across her palm. The intimate contact startled her and she jerked her hand back.

He smiled. She couldn't believe he had the nerve to smile!

"I was wondering if you wanted to join us at Mavis's Diner for supper after we drop off the horses for the night," Kate suggested.

Marni gawked at Kate. This woman—her confidante, her compadre, her ice-cream-and-hot-fudge-at-two-o'clock-in-the-morning-'cause-your-man-ain't-no-good, best pal—was actually trying to set her up. She knew full well how Marni felt about men. You couldn't trust the lot of them because they were only interested in one thing . . . and it wasn't your personality. Of course there were some exceptions, but she doubted Jake was one of them.

"Sure, that'd be great," he said. "We can catch up on the last few years."

"Okay, we'll meet you there around seven," Ben said.

Jake nodded to Kate and Marni as they turned and

walked back to the trailer to see to the horses. "Is your friend coming too?" she heard him say.

Ben answered, "Who, Marni? Yeah, she'll be there."

"Great." She heard something like hands rubbing together.

"Only one problem, Jake."

"What's that?"

"She hates cowboys."

Chapter Two

Marni flopped down on the sofa in her little house. She was exhausted, and it wasn't just from the rodeo. No excuse she used could convince Kate that she didn't want to go tonight. Even after Marni related what had happened at the horse trailer, Kate insisted she would have a good time. In the end it was easier to just agree to dinner.

The phone stared accusingly at her from the end table until she picked it up and dialed her father's number. She really enjoyed talking to him and she loved him a lot, but his constant assertion that he was going to die soon wore her out. Then there was his claim that if she won a championship it would be just like having her mother back again.

Her mother had died before she graduated from high school. Since that sad day her father had been convinced his time was coming. He'd been living with the specter of death for almost fifteen years.

"Hello?" The masculine voice on the other end of the line sounded anything but frail.

"Hi, Dad. How was your week?"

"Tumbleweed! I was wondering if you were going to call your old man or if you'd forgotten about me." At the age of five Marni had decided she wanted to be a gymnast and proved it by doing somersaults all over the yard. Her dad had told her if she failed she could still be a tumbleweed, and the name had stuck.

"You know I wouldn't do that."

"Of course not. Now your brothers I'm not so sure about. With them gallivanting all over the country I'd be surprised if they remember where they live, not to mention their father."

"I'd hardly call it gallivanting. A pilot has to fly and a journalist has to go where the stories are. It's not like they're out chasing a good time. Besides, Troy has a stationary job at the refinery."

"A thousand miles away! A man needs roots," her father argued.

"No. *You* need roots. John, Troy, and Cole need to make a living."

"How was the rodeo today, baby? Did you win?"

"I came in third." And she was sure she would have won if Twister hadn't slipped. "Maybe if you came to watch me ride, you'd bring some good luck. Then I could win."

"You know I'd love to, but you live so far away. Of course, it would be nice to see you before I kick the proverbial bucket. And if you finally won that championship I'd have something to tell your mother when I go to meet her at the pearly gates."

Marni sighed. "It isn't so far if you'd come stay with me for a weekend. There's no ocean between Oklahoma and Texas."

"I can't, I have everything I need right here," her dad

protested. "If the Grim Reaper came to collect me tomorrow, I'd want to be close to my home."

"I don't understand, Dad. Why does that matter?"

"Some of the things I need don't travel well. Like my fifty-year-old bottle of scotch. I don't want to tote it around the countryside."

"When the Reaper finally does come for you, and I don't think it'll be anytime soon, he's not going to sit down and have a drink. Death doesn't work that way. And as far as needing all these things for when you die, you can't take them with you."

"And how would you know that, Tumbleweed? Have you ever died?"

"No, but—"

"Then you can't tell me what it's like."

"Okay, Dad, you win. Now tell me what you did this week."

The conversation continued like any normal father-daughter talk would. It was the same every week. Marni would call and her dad would tell her he was going to die soon. Once they argued about it they were able to talk about what was going on in their lives.

She chatted with her dad and for a short time forgot about her cares, the diner, and the good-looking Peeping Tom.

"What does she mean she doesn't like cowboys?" Jake wondered aloud to the empty booth. He frowned, leaned back into the creaking vinyl bench seat, and stretched his long legs out in front of him, crossing them at the ankles.

"Just what is wrong with cowboys?" He laid one arm across the back of the seat and brooded at the glass door.

Slowly, he drummed his fingers. "And what's wrong with me? I've been told I'm cute."

A waitress walked by and raised an eyebrow at him. He was sure she wondered who he was talking to. Jake ignored her. He stared at the bells that hung from the door, but he only heard someone's silverware clatter, the jukebox lumbering in the background, and the dinner crowd humming with idle chatter.

He turned his thoughts to the horse he had sold that afternoon. Glen Reid was really impressed with the little filly. He had even indicated he might be interested in buying some more stock from him. Goodness knew he needed every sale he could get.

At the rodeo that afternoon a horse trader named Marco Graciani had approached him. He was interested in a deal that would relieve Jake of much of his stock and possibly save his ranch. With his money worries out of the way he would have more energy to spend on other pursuits, like Marni.

Jake snorted. *Yeah, right!* No doubt she had convinced Ben and Kate to stand him up because he was a no-good cowboy.

"Little Jakey Harrison, is that you?" A buxom blonde waitress poured into a bubblegum-pink uniform one size too small stopped by his table and smiled at him. "Gawd, darlin', I haven't seen you in a dog's age."

It took a moment for him to recognize her face before it hit him. "Sally!" There was a time when they had almost been family. "How've you been keeping?"

She plunked down across from him. "I'm just as fat and happy as an old mare out to pasture."

"I'd hardly say you're fat, or old."

"Thanks for noticing, Sugar." She licked her lips and

blatantly checked him out. "You don't look so bad yourself. I see you finally grew into your boots."

He grinned at her. Sally had never been shy about going after what she wanted. "What have you been doing since I last saw you?"

"Well, for starters, I stopped smoking and picked up this addiction instead." She reached into her apron, pulled out a pack of chewing gum, and offered him some, but he refused. After she popped a stick in her mouth she continued, "Mavis is talking about letting me take over the diner so she can retire." She shrugged. "Not much else to tell ya. Cassie moved out to Arizona and is working at a ranch for runaways and troubled teens."

Sally's sister Cassie had been engaged to Jake's brother Tyler until she ran out of the wedding, white skirts flying behind her. Ty never got serious with another woman after her. Jake suspected he was still in love with his fugitive bride, but it wasn't any of his business so he left it alone.

"How about you, Darlin'? What's new and exciting in your life?"

"Let's see . . ." He rubbed his chin and wondered how much he should tell her. The abridged version would do for now. "I moved to Dallas after college, moved back a couple years ago, took over the family ranch, got a serious girlfriend, got rid of the girlfriend, and here I am, end of story."

"Hmmm . . . so the girlfriend situation is—"

"Dismal. I think I have the plague. I got shot down today because I'm a cowboy."

"What's wrong with cowboys?" Sally asked.

"Darned if I know. She's probably just an uptight priss in need of a good—" The words froze on his tongue when he looked down and noticed the three sets of lace-up boots that stood by his table; two small pairs and one large one. A small boot toe tapped furiously on the floor. Jake gulped and looked from the boot to the leg, past the belt buckle, and straight up into Kate's angry eyes.

He glanced to her left and noticed Ben's attempt to suppress a laugh. *No help there.* His eyes darted past Kate to her right and saw Marni's frown. *Aww heck! I did it again.* He returned his attention to Kate and cleared his throat. "Howdy," he croaked.

"Evening," Ben managed to say before breaking into a face-swallowing grin.

Sensing her cue to leave, Sally scooted out of the booth and back to the safety of the kitchen.

Kate grabbed Marni's arm and shoved her into the vacated bench seat across from Jake, plowing in beside her to block any escape attempt. She shot an angry look at her husband that seemed to say she thought he was a traitor and he could sit with the other wart-covered toad.

Ben didn't look as if he noticed as he slid in next to Jake and jostled him over. *So this was how it was going to be. Us against them. The women versus the men.* Jake turned to his still-grinning companion. *We're dead!* He slid deeper into the vinyl seat. It squeaked loudly and earned him the attention of the people who surrounded him.

He gave Marni a weak smile and said quietly, "Heard you did well today. Congratulations."

"Yeah, better than some."

She was entitled to insult him after what she had overheard. Maybe if he put a little effort into it he could smooth her feathers. "Um . . . yeah. So I hear you've only in been in Texas a year. What made you move here?" he asked, in an attempt to lighten the conversation.

Kate and Ben both shook their heads furiously at him. A nerve twitched in Marni's jaw before she covered it.

What did I say now? he wondered.

"I would have thought you'd already heard. I left an ex-fiancé in Oklahoma. He was a rodeo cowboy too." Marni's last comment seemed to be directed right at Jake.

He wanted to smack his forehead. Larry had mentioned a bad relationship. Of course she wouldn't want to talk about it, especially if the guy was so bad she had to move to another state just to get away from him. At least now he knew why she disliked cowboys so much.

The conversation had stuttered to halt, but Jake was saved from further humiliation by the return of Sally.

"How y'all doin' tonight, folks?" Sally snapped her wad of pink gum at them and smiled.

Murmurs of *good* and *fine* went around the table.

"Great! My name's Sally, but you can call me Sal." She winked at Jake, which earned him frowns from the women at the table and an enthusiastic nudge from Ben's elbow. "I'll be your waitress this evening. Now what can I get y'all to drink?"

They placed their orders and Sally handed out menus. She listed the specials, snapping her gum for emphasis after each one, then flashed Jake a brilliant smile and sashayed back toward the kitchen.

"Well, Harrison, you still got your touch. Little ole Sally over there looked more than happy to serve herself up as your main course," Ben said.

Jake heard a crack from under the booth that could only be a boot connecting with the table leg instead of Ben. Kate winced but gave no other indication it was her. He wished he still had his Stetson on so he could pull it down past his eyes and hide until everyone, even Sally went away. "It's not like that, Ben. I know her from before."

Snap. Snap.

Jake looked up to see that Sally had returned to the table with their drinks.

"Here ya go, Sugar." She placed a glass in front of him. "Ice tea, unsweetened with a twist of lemon. I squeezed it myself," she said, winking at him again. She passed out the rest of the drinks without comment.

"Now what can I get y'all to eat?" She pulled her order pad out of her apron and smiled with pen poised in anticipation.

Jake ignored Sally and watched Marni give her order. The sound of her husky voice and the movement of her lips mesmerized him. The irony wasn't lost on him that she was the one woman who had walked into his life that he couldn't charm. In fact, he was sure she hated him for the way he'd acted around her today.

Then she smiled.

Maybe hate was too strong a word. Maybe she even liked him a little bit. He smiled back before he noticed her eyes open wider. She tilted her head toward the outside of the booth. Jake couldn't figure out what was going on.

It hit him. Everyone had made their orders. They were waiting for him to place his while he stared at Marni with a goofy grin on his face.

Jake slid a hand over his eyes and leaned into it. He rested his elbow on the table. "Hamburger, fries, no onions," he mumbled.

"Okay, Honey." He heard Sal walk away from the booth.

"I would have taken you for a guy who likes the works. Someone with a manly appetite and all that," Marni said.

Jake peeked through his fingers at her. She wasn't smiling, but at least she was talking to him.

"I hate onions," he grumbled. He raised his head out of his hand.

"Afraid your breath will scare away any women your charm doesn't?" Marni raised one slim eyebrow and smirked.

"I'm sure my charm doesn't have half the effect the sting of your tongue has," Jake said. Then he shifted uncomfortably. That talk would get him nowhere. *Get a grip, Harrison! If you tried to touch her, she'd knock you flat!*

But her attitude didn't cool his desire. At the moment she looked as tempting as a cool stream after a long day on the trail. Her cheeks were flushed in irritation and she took a deep breath, distracting him before he looked back up at her face. She opened her mouth to speak, but, thank goodness, Sally returned to the table with their meals.

Saved by Sal again. Jake smiled at her. She noticed and gave a little shimmy before she left the table.

Jake's smile turned into a chuckle.

Marni and Kate snorted.

Ben let out a low whistle. "A man could get hypnotized by the sway of those hips."

A sharp kick connected with Jake's shin. He jumped. "Yeow! Kate, you've got to work on your aim!" He rubbed the injured limb and scowled.

Marni tried to suppress a laugh from behind her napkin, but he could see her mirth. Her laughing brown eyes made him want to explore their depths and find new ways to recapture her happiness.

Kate glared at his side of the table. "If you don't like the punishment, you're more than welcome to pass it over to my husband, Jake. Besides, you deserve to share in his blame for encouraging him."

"Encouraging him?" Jake asked. "I haven't said a word!"

"Exactly my point." Kate dug into her meal and didn't say anything else.

Since Ben was suspiciously silent on the subject, Jake was left to try to puzzle out her meaning on his own. He would have said more himself, but he wanted to be able to hobble out of the restaurant on at least one good leg. He picked up his burger and bit deep into it, giving his mouth something else to do besides get him into trouble.

Marni watched Jake behind lowered lashes as she picked at her meal. He kept his eyes on his plate and didn't notice her studying him. A lock of dark brown hair had slid over his forehead; she wondered if it would be as soft as it looked if she reached out and touched it.

Kate had convinced her to come to the diner tonight despite her qualms. She'd told her that they'd known Jake for years and he actually was a nice guy.

"I'm sure what happened this afternoon really was an accident," Kate had said. "Jake's not a Peeping Tom. Besides, I don't think he's needed to sneak a peek since he was a youngster. He's not exactly hard on the eyes, you know."

Kate was right. Marni could hardly stop herself from staring at him. As for that afternoon, she was more embarrassed by the fact that she would rather have beckoned him into the trailer than thrown him out of it. After all, she'd wear less on the beach.

So would he, an evil little voice chimed in her head. A vision of him sun-bronzed in a pair of cutoffs taunted her. Dark hair sprinkled his chest and a smile played around the corners of his mouth before he dove into the water and disappeared. Marni shook herself out of the fantasy.

Men as attractive as Jake Harrison should be kept locked away to protect all of womankind from them. Marni stabbed a fry as an image of Jake, locked in a bedroom for her pleasure, flooded her mind. Her fork crashed onto the plate and skidded across the surface. It made a sound like fingernails on a chalkboard. She shivered, but wasn't sure if it was from the sound or the images swimming in her head.

"You don't have to kill them. They're already dead," Jake remarked before he returned his attention to his food.

Marni glanced at the fry dangling on her fork. It was skewered in the middle and pushed right up to the top. She plucked it off with her fingers and popped it in her mouth. Idly, she licked off a blob of ketchup that was left on her thumb.

She heard a cough from across the table.

Marni's eyes snapped up and she realized Jake was staring at her mouth. She nipped at the pad of her thumb, then smiled. Wickedly. He glanced up at her and his cough turned into a strangled choke. He grabbed his glass of iced tea and took a gulp before he set it down. He coughed again and Ben walloped him between his shoulder blades.

Hard.

Jake wore a pained expression. He appeared to be lost in his own personal agony.

Maybe Ben had dislocated his shoulder?

"Aw heck, Benth! I biwth my towngue!" He struggled to make himself understood.

"What?" Marni asked.

"I think he said he bit his tongue," Kate offered.

Jake nodded.

Ben grabbed the glass of iced tea and swung around to give it to Jake. "Here, maybe some ice will—"

The cool liquid sloshed into Jake's lap. He tried to avoid it and cracked his elbow on the table's edge, making him double over in pain.

"—help" Ben finished lamely.

Both women flinched in sympathy.

Jake sat up, clenching his jaw.

Marni finally found her voice. "Are you all right?"

"Maybe you should let him out of the booth, Ben," Kate suggested, trying to be helpful. She made a sweeping gesture with her hands to get her husband to move.

Ben shot out of the stall and Jake slid out behind him.

When he turned around Marni noticed he had the broadest shoulders any man should be allowed to have. The muscles tapered down to slim hips. Tight jeans covered his lower body like a fitted cover over a mattress.

As Jake made his cautious way around Ben and walked toward the restrooms, Marni noticed a slight limp. In less than an hour Kate and Ben had dealt him more injuries than he would get after a day at the rodeo.

Nurse Sally, a.k.a. Sal the Waitress, scurried after Jake to the men's room. There was no doubt she meant to offer her services to the injured cowboy. Marni could imagine what she would say: "I prescribe two aspirins and then go straight to my bed, Sugarcakes."

Yuck!

Ben sat in the booth and grumbled, "The way he's carrying on you'd think I tried to kill him or something." The hangdog expression on his face said more than his words did.

"Honey, he knows you didn't do it on purpose," Kate

comforted. "Besides, I think you hurt his pride more than his person."

Ben perked up. "Maybe I should go check on him?"

"I think you should just wait. The bill will be here soon and after tonight we both owe him dinner."

Ben nodded and settled back in the booth.

"Well, if we're waiting, then I'm hitting the ladies' room," Marni said. "Scoot over, Kate. Let me out." As she strode toward the facilities, she noticed Sally was back on duty behind the counter.

I guess ol' Sugarcakes didn't need her help after all. Marni didn't know why that made her happy.

Jake checked his tongue in the mirror. *Yup, still there. I didn't bite it off.*

When Ben had slapped his shoulder blades, he thought he'd bit it clean through. But now he wasn't even sure if he was bleeding.

He considered the kind of day he'd had and realized it had all started with Marni. He gave himself a mental shake. The last time a girl had caused him so much pain he was fourteen. He remembered trying to impress Missy Taylor when he was on the high school rodeo circuit. He'd swung his lariat and threatened to rope her and make her his own.

Missy got away just fine. Too bad Jake couldn't say the same for George Talbot's rusty fender. When the truck had pulled away, it'd pulled Jake with it. He'd gone face first into the dirt and was dragged along in a trail of dust. Jake's weight had been too much for the old fender. With a groan, the aged piece of metal had ripped free of the truck frame.

For weeks after the mishap he was known as Junkyard Jake. If you needed a part, he could rope it for you. It took a long time for him to live that down. Far longer than it took the rub burns on his arms to heal.

Jake didn't want to relive his teenage angst at his age. The best thing he could do was leave Marni alone, especially since she was becoming his personal bad-luck charm. If only she wasn't so cute.

He left the bathroom, and as fate would have it, ran straight into Marni coming out of the ladies' room. He was instantly aware of her body as he slammed into her in the cramped hall. Her soft curves fit perfectly against him. He steadied her by her shoulders and glared down. "That seals it! You're a jinx!"

"Pardon me?" She looked up at him, one slim eyebrow raised. "I am not! You're the one who's made a mess of himself all evening. Now you come crashing into the hallway and try to blame *me* for *your* clumsiness!"

"That's right, Darlin'. I didn't have a problem until this morning. It started right after I met you."

"So it's my fault?"

"Yup." Jake slid past Marni in the narrow hall and headed back to the booth. He could hear her scramble to keep up with him.

"Did you hit your head too?"

Jake stopped at the table. He glanced at her. A slight flush was creeping up from her chest to her neck. "No, Marni, my head is fine. You were the beginning of all my problems; therefore, *you* are the problem. A jinx, plain and simple."

"I am not!" Marni protested. Her eyes flared and the fire in them stirred a smile from Jake. It was her passion that got to him.

"Now children," Ben spoke up, "if you don't settle down we'll send you home without dessert."

"I *want* to go home!" Jake and Marni declared in unison.

Kate crossed her arms over her chest and looked at them sternly. "Go home then. Jake, you know where we live, you can drop Marni off on your way."

"On my way? Your place isn't on my way."

"I'm *not* going home with *him*."

"Besides, I'm not letting that woman in my truck. If my luck holds, I'll get in some freak accident on the way home. She won't have a scratch, but I'll break every bone in my body."

"I couldn't fit in that truck with his great big ego, even if I did agree to go with him. Which I haven't."

"I do not have a swelled head. I've been stating scientific fact," Jake asserted.

Ben scratched at the day's growth on his chin and sighed, drawing everyone's attention. "You know, I've been thinking of selling my Doc-bred mare. Her daddy was a world champion roping horse."

"You mean Dusty?" Jake asked. "I've wanted that broodmare since she was a filly in your field. She's a beauty."

"Of course, I might breed her to Ed Patrick's stud," Ben said, still scratching his chin and inclining his head suggestively toward Marni.

Jake took the hint. "You're blackmailing me?"

"I prefer to call it incentive." Ben grinned.

Kate smiled at her husband.

"Fine, I'll take Marni home, but you two are responsible for my hospital bill."

"We're already paid for your dinner, don't push it," Kate teased him.

"Excuse me," Marni interrupted. "I'm not a bag of grain to be bartered with. I have an opinion. What if he drops me at the side of the road in the middle of nowhere and makes me walk?"

"I said I'll take you home and I will."

Marni snorted.

Jake turned to Kate and asked, "Do you still have a long driveway?"

"You see!" Marni exclaimed. "Your driveway has to be a mile long!"

"I *could* breed Dusty to Kurt Laudin's stud," Ben mused, feigning intense interest in the subject. "What do you think, Kate?"

Jake threw up his hands. "Okay, okay! I'll take her all the way home."

"To the bunkhouse?" Kate asked.

"To the bunkhouse. Right at the steps of the bunkhouse. Safe and sound," Jake promised.

"Good," Ben said. "Maybe I *will* sell my horse to you, Harrison." He winked at his wife. "We'll talk."

Jake looked at Marni. Her fists were balled up and resting on her hips. She glowered at the bunch of them. "You're pretty quiet for someone with an opinion," he said.

"There's no sense arguing with them," she grumbled. "They'll come up with an excuse for anything I say."

"You look tired. You should go to bed." Kate smiled.

"You have to work early in the morning," Ben added. "You shouldn't stay up too late."

"Come on, let's go." Jake led a reluctant Marni to his beat-up blue pickup truck.

He couldn't resist one last jab so he said, "You have to get in on the driver's side, the passenger's door is wired shut." In truth there was nothing wrong with either door, but once the idea formed he couldn't resist the urge to aggravate her a little more.

Marni eyed his truck. "Are you sure this thing will get us both home?"

"She's not pretty, but she has a strong motor and gets me where I need to go. Plus, the air conditioning works." Jake started to open the door but stopped when someone ran up behind him calling his name.

"Jake, Honey, you forgot something," Sally purred.

"Huh?" Jake turned around and was pressed up against the truck door by Sally. This was getting tiring, but he couldn't be rude. He looked at Marni and noticed she stood back, watching with her arms crossed and a slight frown creasing her brow.

"My phone number, Sugar. Call me." She tucked a slip of paper in his breast pocket, kissed him full on the lips, and slid down his chest. She sashayed back to the diner and turned once to blow him a kiss.

Jake ignored it and opened the door of his truck. "Your carriage awaits, Ma'am." He swept his arm past the opening and bowed slightly at the waist.

Marni huffed and climbed into the truck. Jake put his hands on her shapely hips to steady her but snatched them back when she snapped at him.

"Take your paws off me, you pig!"

"Pigs don't have paws, Darlin'. And I was just helping you get in." He slid in beside her.

"Copping a feel is more like it."

"I was not!" Jake cried in mock horror. He started the engine and asked, "So Marni, why am I a pig?"

She glared at him. "One moment you're snuggling up to that waitress, and then as soon as she's out of sight you're grabbing for me."

"Actually, *she* was snuggling up to *me*." Jake backed up his pickup and pulled out of the parking lot.

"And another thing," she went on. "How did she know that I wasn't your girlfriend, or your wife for that matter?"

"Well, you didn't slug her, for one." He grinned at her before he continued, "I really do know her. We were talking before you came in. Does this mean you're jealous?"

"No!"

He glanced at Marni and she blushed, then wrapped both arms tight around her waist and looked out the passenger's window.

After a few minutes of silence, Jake leaned forward to play with the radio. He brushed Marni's arm on purpose as he reached for the tuning knob. She jumped and glared at him.

"Do I make you nervous?" he asked.

"You mean besides your driving? Can't you keep your eyes on the road?" She rubbed her arm where they'd touched as if she'd been burned.

A shock of awareness had jolted through Jake's body when he'd touched her. Even now he still tingled from wrist to shoulder.

Seems like more than your temper is electric. I wonder what else is? Jake shut the thought down before it could go any further.

He drummed his fingertips against the steering wheel and stared at the road, eventually pulling into Kate and Ben's long drive. Turn Around Ranch sat far back from the highway. Pastureland ran down both sides of the driveway, and he could see squat lean-tos in the distance and the outlines of a few horses left out to graze.

The sun had just gone down and dusk was making a rapid descent into dark. Jake rolled past the sprawling farmhouse to the small bunkhouse near the barn. At one time it might have lodged the cook and ranch foreman, but now it was Marni's home. Both front windows held sill pots over-flowing with flowers. He could just make out the lacy white curtains that sheltered Marni from the outside world. He drove up to the first step of the front porch.

"Here we are. Right at your front steps, just like I promised." He turned in the seat and smiled at her.

"Are you going to let me out of the truck, or do you expect me to climb out over top of you?"

"I'll even hold the door for you . . . for a price."

A shocked expression crossed her face before she turned toward the window and quickly rolled it down. In one smooth motion she pulled herself out of the truck and dropped onto the ground like she'd never had the need to use a door in her life. She leaned into the window and made a face at him.

"What? No good-night kiss?" he asked.

She growled and stomped up the porch steps.

Jake leaned out her window. "By the way, Marni." She turned back and he hesitated. He really should give her a break, but common sense was overruled by the urge to give her one last push. "The passenger door isn't broken." He opened and shut the door to prove his point.

"Then why say it was?"

"Guess I couldn't resist a chance to see you wiggle out of the window."

"*You*," Marni glared at him, "are a rat!" She whipped into the house and slammed the door so hard the welcome sign bounced off its nail onto the planks below.

"And *you* have the spirit of an untamed filly. I'd love to find new ways to get you to show it," Jake said into the quiet night air.

He wondered why would he want to spend more time with Marni as he drove home. Back at the diner he'd made up his mind to stay away from her. He'd even thought she was a bit of bad luck he just didn't need right now. But no jinx had ever aroused such passion in him before.

Then there was Sally. She'd charged into the men's room after him with a proposition to help. She'd brought him ice for his limp, cooed and offered to kiss things better whether they needed to be kissed or not. She'd been all soft curves and femininity pressed against him—and he'd felt nothing.

Jake took out the piece of paper Sally had tucked into his pocket. It had red lipstick marks on it and smelled of perfume. He smiled and let it flutter out the window. It looked like a white feather as it disappeared into the darkness.

"Sorry, Sally."

Chapter Three

Marni stared at the white plaster ceiling of her bedroom. At 4:00 A.M. she'd given up trying to sleep and now lay in bed waiting for dawn to arrive.

She'd spent the last hour thinking up creative ways to kill Jake. Impalement on a cactus, hanging him by his spurs, or her personal favorite, stampeding him with his disgruntled ex-lovers on horseback. Even this activity didn't help her, because when she *had* slept she'd dreamt of Jake.

She'd hoped to envision his untimely demise or at least serious maiming of some of his more vital body parts. Instead, her dreams had been filled with his body, his kisses, and his electric touch. He'd consumed her senses.

Marni threw her pillow across the room. It thumped harmlessly against the wall and slid to the floor. "Okay, so I hate everything about you except for your body," Marni accused. "That's not saying much. A lump of clay can be formed into a beautiful sculpture. It doesn't mean there's any more substance to it than mud." But no lump of clay ever kept her up at night, or sent shivers of awareness spiraling up her arm from a casual touch.

She slid a damp curl off her forehead. The ceiling fan did little to dispel the heat in the room. Ben and Kate had offered to install an air conditioner in the bunkhouse, but she didn't want them to go to any more trouble for her. They'd already done so much.

They'd taken Marni and Twister in without question when she showed up at the ranch a year ago looking for a place to stay. She couldn't stand to spend another minute in Oklahoma, so she didn't move in with her father. Instead, she packed her bags, borrowed a horse trailer, and headed out to the Turn Around Ranch in an attempt to turn her own life around. Kate was Marni's old baby-sitter and accepted the role of caretaker again without question. Ben and Kate refused to take any money for keeping Twister, and Marni argued with them for the right to pay her own room and board.

She'd only gotten a few hours' rest and knew she would be a groggy mess at work. Sleeplessness didn't help her bad temper much either. Marni got out of bed, ran cold water over her wrists, and splashed some on her face to cool down. She looked in the mirror and thought about how lucky she was to have two such good friends. *They never asked me what happened, they just waited patiently until I was ready to tell them. They even called Roy a few choice names for my sake and then never brought him up again.*

Marni toweled off and laid back down on top of the bed, but when she looked at the clock blinking 5:30 at her, she knew if she started now she could feed the horses for Kate and shower before she left for work. Yawning, she hauled herself off the bed. *Now I know how roosters must feel. Of*

*course, they can go back to bed after they wake up every-
one else.*

She dressed in a pair of torn jeans and an ancient T-shirt,
thought about running a brush through her short curls, but
opted for a baseball cap instead. The horses didn't care
what she looked like. Her worn sneakers were her favorite
piece of clothing and she wiggled her toes in delight after
she slid them on.

When she left the house, she noticed her welcome sign
on the porch floor. It hadn't suffered any damage from last
night's fall. Marni was glad for that, but she would have
sacrificed the sign for a chance to break it over Jake's head.
*Who am I kidding? He'd never feel the plywood crack
through his thick skull.*

Marni glanced around the ranch and noticed that the first
rays of the sun were breaking over the horizon. She
bounded down the front steps and strode across the yard to
the battered old green pickup Kate used for feeding the
horses. The keys were stashed in the glove compartment.
Marni dug them out and set the truck rumbling to life. She
pulled it up to the back of the barn and turned it off before
taking the wheelbarrow to the storage shed, which con-
sisted of a roof on support beams.

She threw some bales down from the top of the pile for
the horses and climbed back down. She took some of them
into the barn with the wheelbarrow and threw the rest into
the bed of her truck. In the feed room, using a large scoop,
she measured out grain rations into pails. The dust from
the oats made her sneeze. Marni put the food into the truck
and drove out into the first, pitted field.

The horses galloped up to meet her and followed the
vehicle to the lean-tos where they were fed. When she got
out of the truck, insistent muzzles pushed at the food.

"Okay, guys," she giggled, "I'll feed you, I promise."
She dumped grain into troughs around the building and
checked the automatic waterers to make sure they were
clean and working.

After Marni fed all of the pasture horses, she parked the
truck and proceeded to feed the animals in the barn. Kate
and Ben kept their broodmares with new foals inside, along
with their rodeo stock. These horses went out after their
breakfast and came back in before dinner.

Playing favorites, Marni fed Twister first. "Morning,
Baby. How are you feeling today?" she asked her sweet
gelding.

"Just fine, thanks," a deep, familiar voice rumbled from
behind her.

Startled, Marni spun around to stare into Jake's smiling
eyes. She caught her breath. He looked devastating in the
early morning light. His hair was freshly washed and
combed. No hat adorned his head. His jaw was clean-
shaven, and like she had noticed the day before, his teeth
gleamed. Marni was uncomfortably aware of her own appearance.

"Whatareyoudoinghere?" Caught off guard, her words
ran together. She inhaled deeply and the next time she
asked her question it came out clearly. "I mean, what are
you doing here?"

"I thought Kate and Ben were in the barn when I saw
the doors open. I didn't mean to alarm you."

"They're in the house." Marni went back to her chores.
She hoped the distracting cowboy would go away.

"Which one's yours?"

No such luck; he wasn't leaving. "The tall bay I was
talking to when you walked in."

Jake strolled over to her horse and peeked in on the contentedly-munching gelding. The horse ignored him.

"Twister's social until he's distracted by food." He didn't even lift his head out of his breakfast when she said his name.

Marni continued with her chores. She lifted Dusty's hay over the double door. She stifled the urge to jump when Jake reached over her shoulder to stroke the mare. He stood so close behind Marni that she could feel his T-shirt brushing her own.

When he spoke to the horse, his voice came out as a low purr. "One of these days, Beautiful, you're going to be mine."

With Jake's voice so close to her ear, Marni could imagine he was saying those words to her. She wanted to sink back into his chest and lose herself in his warmth. She almost forgot he wanted the horse, not her. *Have you completely lost your mind? You were thinking of creative ways to murder him a couple of hours ago.*

She jolted herself upright. "Do you mind?" she snapped. "I have things to do before I go to work."

"Work?" He stepped back and grinned. "Where do you work? Not in public relations, I hope."

"I work in a bank."

"With people? Tell me you don't treat them the same way you treat me. I'm a tough guy, I can take it but some poor old lady . . ." Jake shook his head, ". . . you could ruin her whole day.

"For your information, I like most people. It's *you* I can't stand," Marni fumed.

"Funny," Jake mulled, "I get along with most everyone. Why wouldn't you like me? Is it because you're—"

"So it's back to this again. Well, let me tell you, I'm not

any of the things you accuse me of being. I'm not a jinx!
I'm not mean to people! I'm not anything else you might
think of! It's you! I just don't like you!" *I want you....*

Stop that! She berated herself.

"I didn't say you were mean," Jake stated.

"What were you going to call me?" Marni asked self-
consciously.

"Spirited," he said, then smiled. "Wilder than an untamed filly and twice the fun."

"No!" She put her hands on her hips. "I don't want to
hear this. I want you to leave me alone!"

He chuckled at her. "Can't do that, Marni."

"Why?" She wanted to holler and stomp her feet much
like the filly he compared her to. "Last night you said you
didn't want me anywhere near you."

"Well, the way I see it . . ." Jake walked a slow circuit
around her. "If a doctor has a patient with an unknown
illness, he doesn't run away screaming. He examines the
patient and the affliction until he finds a cure." Jake stopped
in front of her and eyed her critically with his chin captured
between his thumb and index finger. His left hand rested
at his waist where his thumb was hooked through one of
the belt loops.

"So instead of running scared, like last night," Marni
raised an eyebrow at Jake and dared him to take the bait,
"you've decided that I'm a disease and you have to figure
me out."

"You drove the nail into the shoe, Darlin'. I need to stick
real close to you until I figure out why disaster strikes me
when you're around." The smile he gave her was slow and
seductive, leaving no room to misinterpret his intent.
" 'Course, nothing's happened this morning."

Marni chose to ignore that. "Aren't you afraid the research is going to be hazardous to your health?" Her hands crept from her waist to cross over her chest. The gesture was more for protection against the feelings this man invoked than from anger toward him.

"It's a sacrifice I'm willing to make in the name of science. The discovery is worth the risk." This time Jake raised his eyebrows in challenge.

"I have no interest in being your scientific discovery, conquest, or otherwise, Jake Harrison. It's bad enough that we live in the same state together, but now you've decided to stick to me like a burr to a horse's tail and be just as provocative."

"Mmm, provocative. I like that. How else would you describe me?" His eyes smoldered with suggestion.

"You know what I mean! You're a pain in the—"

"Now, now, play nice," Jake whispered and approached, "or I might have to retaliate."

Marni felt like a wildcat was stalking her and she'd just run into a blind canyon. Every backward step was matched by his advance. His movements were as sinuous as the cat he resembled, and his eyes were as dangerous. Dappled sunlight filtered through the barn boards and danced in his hair and across his face. It played with the shadows there and added to his mystery.

The rough wood of the barn wall grated against Marni's back and she knew she was caught. Trapped in the spell of predator and prey, she now understood how deer that stood in a trance, waiting for the deathblow, felt. All of her senses were focused on Jake. The smell of horses and hay disappeared into the smell of his cologne. Her gaze locked on his face and she lost sight of the barn. He was so close, yet she could barely hear his slow, steady breathing over the thunder of her heart. Her skin tingled in anticipation of his touch and her tongue ached to taste him.

Jake stopped short of touching her and swept off her tattered baseball cap instead. Marni reached up to worry her tangled curls, but he dropped her hat and took hold of her fingers before she could touch her hair. With his other hand he caressed her cheek, tracing her jawline from ear to chin. Where he touched her, she felt branded. He tilted up her head and searched her face.

He's going to kiss me. Fear raced through her veins, along with want and need. Desire confused her common sense. *And I'm going to let him.*

She knew she should run out of the barn, slap him or something, but her legs stayed rooted to the spot and her arms refused to push him away. A whimper escaped her as he lowered his lips to hers.

Somewhere through the web that Jake had woven around her, she heard someone's throat clear. Marni's head snapped sideways out of Jake's grasp. She saw Ben standing in the doorway, discreetly eyeing the ceiling beams. Anger and embarrassment fought inside of her. She was mad at herself for letting Jake draw her in. She dropped her gaze and noticed her baseball cap lying crumpled and spiritless on the concrete floor, much like her pride.

Marni ducked to pick up the cap and hide her reddened cheeks. How could she be so stupid? She knew better than to trust another man so easily. Jake would treat her just like Roy had. He'd be charming and sweet until he knew he could manipulate her. After that, she would just be another notch on his bedpost. She snatched her cap off the floor and beat the dust off with one hard smack against her leg. She jammed it back on her head, pushed past Jake, and strode over to Ben.

"The horses in the pasture are fed, but some of them in here are still waiting for their breakfast. I'm going to shower before work."

"Thanks." Ben accepted her statement without demanding any explanation of what had happened.

Marni started to leave the barn but turned back when Jake spoke up.

"Need someone to scrub your back?"

"Need someone to peel your *hide*?" she retorted as she left. When she was away from the barn, she ran for the safety of her house, sprinted up the front steps, wrenched the door open, and slammed it shut behind her. Acting as if Jake was at her heels, she hurried to her bedroom. Leaning against that door once she closed it she released a heavy breath, then dragged herself over to the closet.

She took the clothes she needed into the bathroom, stripped down, and turned on the shower. When the water warmed to a comfortable temperature, she stepped in.

Marni felt she deserved a cold shower for the way she had behaved. She couldn't believe she had fallen for his act. She scrubbed roughly at her skin, but she couldn't erase the memory of Jake, nor the hum of excitement she felt whenever he was close.

Jake followed Ben, waiting for him to say something, anything.

Either he's going to yell at me and tell me to stay away from her, or he'll slap me on the back, call me an old dog, and tell me to go after her.

"How's Sally?" Ben asked casually.

"Sally?"

"Yeah, 'but you can call me Sal.' " Ben winked.

"I know who you're talking about, but why would I know how she is?"

"Well, you two seemed pretty cozy in the parking lot last night."

Ben didn't need to say anything more. Jake knew what he was getting at. "How do you know about that? Did Marni say something?" He sounded defensive even to his own ears.

"We could see your truck from the window in the booth. I had to hold onto Kate so she wouldn't run to the parking lot and scratch Sally's eyes out."

"Oh." Jake looked down at his scuffed boots. "I threw Sally's number away, if that means anything."

"Hmmm." Ben turned his back and got one of the horses ready to go outside. Before he took the horse out he said, "It's Marni's story to tell, but I will say there is a good reason she ran from Oklahoma."

"You mean the fiancé?"

"Hmmm," was the only answer he got before Ben left him standing alone in the barn.

Frustrated, Jake ran both hands through his hair. He spun on his boot heel and looked at the horses in the barn. "Can any of you tell me what *hmmm* is supposed to mean?" But none of them answered.

Ben came back in and Jake helped him put out the rest of the horses. When the barn was empty, they got to the real reason he had come.

"I'm guessing you're here to talk about that mare?" Ben asked. He sat on one of the hay bales against the wall. "She's a looker."

"I've wanted Dusty for a long time and you know that, but there's a problem." Jake leaned against the wall and crossed his arms. "When my mom and dad retired and gave the ranch to me, I knew it would be hard to bring it back into working order. I had hoped I could convince my brother or sister to operate it with me, but they both refused. At the time I had a large chunk of money saved up from my marketing job. I thought that was enough, but . . ."

"Go on."

"Well, I started seeing Carol-Anne. It got pretty serious and she moved in with me. She's the type of woman who likes to be kept and can run through a guy's savings like water. When the money was gone, so was she."

Ben nodded. "So she used you to keep her nails buffed and her hair curled, then left you flat."

"Her leaving me like that was bad, but it was a blessing and the least of my problems."

"How bad are we talking?" Ben rested his shoulders against the stall wall and pushed his feet out in front of him.

"If I don't sell a lot of horses real soon, I'm going to have to consider other options."

A whistle escaped Ben's teeth.

"Tell me about it," Jake said. "I don't want to sell the ranch and I don't want to go back to work full time, but the contract work I've been doing for my old company isn't enough to pay the bills anymore. They've offered me a full-time position, but I want to be outside, not sitting behind a desk."

"I feel for you, buddy. Being cooped up in the high walls of a city must have chafed at your cowboy pride. I know there are days I'd rather be working on the farm than in an office," Ben said.

"On a better note, I do have a buyer interested in my horses. Marco Graciani. Heard of him?"

"No, is he a horse trader or something?"

"Yeah. He claims that signing on with him would mean having a contact for selling all my horses. The only hitch is that he wants first pick of each year's crop." Jake crinkled his brow in thought. "I've been trying to negotiate with him on that. I have other clients to consider, even if they don't buy many horses."

"Sounds like you got things under control."

"Let's hope so. I'm okay so long as the house isn't relocated by a tornado, the well doesn't go dry, and the barn doesn't burn down," he joked.

Ben got up and walked out of the barn to the corral where Dusty sedately munched her hay. Jake followed him out. He put his foot on the bottom rail of the fence and leaned his arms on the top. The warm morning promised a hot day, but a light breeze offered some forgiveness from the heat. He looked over his shoulder at the rest of the farm and noticed that Marni's car was already gone.

"So what are we going to do about this horse?"

Ben's question brought Jake's attention back to the corral and the pretty chestnut mare with the big brown eyes. "It's not fair of me to ask this from you, and I'll understand if you say no. I was hoping you would keep her for awhile. At least until I know whether or not I'm going to sign on with Graciani. Neither one of us would breed her until the springtime anyway."

"I think we can do better than that." Ben picked at the paint peeling off the fence post.

"I'd pay you now, but I have the men's wages to consider." The check he'd gotten from Glen Reid was too small to cover the wages.

"You don't understand what I'm trying to say, Jake. We only hire temporary ranch hands because the operation is so small. It's more a hobby than an occupation. The thing is, with me living and working in Houston most of the week, a lot of the chores don't get done. Kate and Marni take care of the horses and I'm supposed to do the farm maintenance."

Jake decided he liked what Ben was saying to him. He'd get the horse and get to spend plenty of time with Marni too. "So you want me to paint fences, do repairs, and stuff like that? In exchange you'll give me Dusty?"

"That's what I'm suggesting."

"You've got a deal!" Jake stepped off the fence rail and shook Ben's hand.

"If you two are done jawing, I've got coffee," Kate called from the side porch of the main house.

The men went inside and took their boots off in the entrance. They padded softly on sock feet over the hardwood floor to sit at the dining table. The strong aroma of coffee almost covered the subtler scent of lemon polish. The room gleamed with morning sunlight shining through the open windows. Lacy blue half-curtains the complemented the small-blue-flower dotted, cream-colored wallpaper.

"Looks like you boys were making a deal out there. Anything I should be concerned about?" Kate placed a steaming mug in front of each man, then went back into the kitchen for her own.

"Just that Jake has agreed to be your own personal slave."

Kate sat down at the table with the two men. "Oooh . . . I like the sound of that. You didn't tell me we were getting a new stud on the farm. When did you say you were leaving for Houston, Honey?" Kate winked at Jake.

"Hey, hey! There'll be none of that. He'll be doing hard labor only. And he's not allowed anywhere near the hay barn."

"Well, dang it, Ben," Jake teased. "I thought I'd get to take care of all your farm duties. If Kate's not part of the deal, I'm not sure I'm interested."

"Kate, where's my shotgun?"

As they talked about Kate and Ben's plans for the ranch, Jake's mind wandered to soft skin, brown eyes, and chestnut curls. As soon as he could, he steered the conversation to a topic that burned in his mind.

"Marni mentioned she works in a bank. Which one?" Jake tried to make the question sound innocent, but he was sure they knew how obvious he was.

"I don't think we should tell you after the way you acted yesterday," Kate said. "I could barely drag her to the diner. She was pretty adamant about the whole pervert thing, then we walk in on you trying to be a comedian. And that episode with Sally in the parking lot was enough to steam my cold tea."

"Oh yeah." Jake fingered the neckline of his T-shirt. "Did I say I was sorry about that?"

"No, and I bet you didn't say as much to Marni either," Kate pressed.

"Well, no." The cozy little room suddenly felt suffocating and hot.

"There's only one bank in Okida," Kate said. "That's the one she works at. But, before you go racing over there to bother her, remember that your life is in my hands now."

Jake considered the plan he had made. He intended to draw Marni out by being near her as much as possible. No doubt that was going to bug her, and Kate would side with Marni, not him. He'd have to be careful. "Yes, Ma'am," he said.

"Guess you have a bank account to open. Better get to it," Ben said.

"Thanks for the coffee," Jake said. He kissed Kate on the cheek and left.

"Can I help the next customer?" Marni called. She glanced at the line of bank patrons and looked back down at the paperwork on her work space without seeing it.

"I was wondering if I could deposit some money into my bank account, Darlin'."

The smooth drawl caused Marni's head to snap up. She locked eyes with the pair of deep blue ones across from her. "What?"

"My account?" Jake prompted. "I want to put money in it. This is a bank, right?"

Marni watched the mischievous smile spread across his face. Could it really be she'd only known him two days? It felt more like an eternity. In hell.

"Marni?" Jake waved his hand past her eyes. "I *can* deposit money in my account, right?"

"Of course. But why do you have an account here? Kate said you live in Meridian. It can't be convenient." Marni knew how rude she sounded. She was tired and muddled from her lack of sleep and her early morning encounter with Jake. She didn't want to have to deal with him right now.

Jake handed her his bankbook. "Actually, it's really convenient."

Marni waited for an explanation, but he didn't say anything. She looked at her watch. *Eleven o'clock. Darn!* She had already taken her break and it was too early for lunch. "Okay, I'll ask. Why here?"

"You don't know? I'm doing some work for Ben," he said. "I'll be at his farm an awful lot, real late too, so I had to open an account in case I need some quick cash."

A loud groan escaped Marni. The teller at the next station threw a curious glance her way. Jake working at the farm would be as much fun for her as fire ants in her jeans. "Haven't you ever heard of a bank machine?"

"Oh sure, but I prefer personal service."

Frustrated, Marni opened the forgotten bankbook. It looked suspiciously new. In fact, when she checked the first entry date and confirmed it with the wall calendar, it was the same day. "You opened this today?"

He nodded.

"Why didn't you put in your full deposit then?" She sounded like a shrew, but she didn't care. The man was trying to drive her mad.

"And miss seeing my favorite bank teller? Never." He winked at her.

She stifled the urge to throw her rubber stamp at him and carefully asked him for his deposit. He handed her five crisp twenty-dollar bills that had probably come from the bank machine out front. The worm. She made up a deposit slip and slid it toward him.

"Sign here, initial here," she said as sweetly as she could. He didn't need to know how much he bothered her.

Jake raised an eyebrow at her. "I almost think you're starting to warm up to me, Marni."

"Not likely." She snatched the signed slip out of his fingertips and stamped it with a loud, punctuating thud. The tellers and clients closest to her jumped and cast startled looks her way.

Jake chuckled at her, and when she glared up at him he shrugged his shoulders and pointed at the slip. "I think you missed a spot."

She growled and put his book in the machine to be updated, then handed it to him and watched as he slid it back into the plastic sleeve. "Why me?" she asked. "Of all the people you could chose to aggravate, why me?"

"Because," he looked at her, "you're the only woman I know who doesn't like me."

"You're kidding, right? There must be an ex-girlfriend or two who never want to see you again."

"Nope." He didn't even hesitate to answer. "I get along with all my ex-girlfriends."

Darn, there goes that fantasy. "So if I throw myself at your feet and beg for your attention, you'll lose interest and leave me alone?" Marni asked hopefully.

"That'd be a nice place to start. I demand *a lot* of attention." His voice was slow, sexy, and suggestive. "But you wouldn't lose my interest that quickly. I'd have to have my way with you first." A smile quirked his lips before he got it under control. "When do you want to start?"

Marni swallowed. She felt a blush creep hotly up her cheeks. "How about the day after I teach Twister to tap-dance?" she croaked. She couldn't believe the gall of the man. Even Roy wasn't that cocky.

"Consider it a date." Jake tipped his hat at her and sauntered out the door.

Marni gaped at his retreating back until old Mrs. Phillips cleared her throat. "My, my, what a handsome man. Big feet."

"They counterbalance his big head," Marni retorted.

Chapter Four

Jake's truck was gone when she got home from work. She had successfully avoided him since Monday by coming home late every day from the bank. Some of her friends were starting to wonder about her sudden obsession with diner food. Sally now knew her by name.

The Friday Night Mason Jar Rodeo was today and that meant that Marni couldn't avoid Jake for much longer. He would be there with his horse, waiting to pounce on her. She made her way down the steps and out to the barn. The hot day had cooled into a pleasant evening. The air smelled of rain and Marni was sure they wouldn't make it through the whole weekend without a downpour.

In the barn, Kate and Ben had already fed the horses. Kate's mare, Angel, waited on the crossties while she was brushed and had her legs wrapped for the trailer. Her owner smiled at Marni. "Evenin', Stranger, wondered if you were ever coming out of that house."

"I had to change and eat and do stuff before we left."

"Never known you to take so long to do that, is all."

Marni cleared her throat to buy her time while she thought of a response. "I was pretty tired after work. I must be moving slower tonight."

"Yeah, uh-huh." Kate looked at Marni in disbelief. "Hope your horse isn't having the same problem. If you're going for the championship, then you're going to have to score some points."

"I'll need more than a little speed to win that buckle." Marni went to her horse's stall and led him out. "I'll need a whole lot of luck too."

"I'm not so sure. You work hard with Twister, and the two of you make a great team. I honestly believe this is your year."

"I can only hope."

In no time they were ready and had their horses loaded in the trailer. Ben slid in behind the steering wheel with Kate beside him. Marni jumped into the back seat of the blue-and-silver crew-cab truck. They rumbled down the drive and out onto the highway before Ben spoke up.

"I'll be leaving for Houston on Monday and I won't be back until late Friday night. You girls call Jake if you need anything."

"We're not frightened children, Ben. Marni and I have been taking care of the place on our own for a year," Kate admonished.

"Besides, Kate's a sharp shot with your shotgun. I wouldn't suggest you sneak up on her while she's holding it," Marni teased.

"Okay. I get the point. You're two self-sufficient ladies. You don't need me or any man to take care of you. Should I even bother to come home again?"

"Of course, Honey. There are some things men are useful

for." Kate put her hand on Ben's leg. "Like killing spiders." She turned around and looked at Marni. "Isn't that right?"

"Absolutely. And opening jars, and taking out the garbage."

"I can see I'm outnumbered. I'll shut up now."

"That's how I like my man, silent and obedient." Kate gave her husband a pat on the knee that earned a grunt from him.

The banter continued all the way to the rodeo arena, and Marni forgot about Jake until they pulled in. Then she saw his truck and horse trailer from the entrance. He stood beside his horse, waving them into the spot next to him. *Oh great!* Not only would she be unable to avoid him, She'd be parked right beside him. *I should've taken the horse trailer too when I left Roy.*

Ben parked the trailer and Marni slunk out of the truck, unsuccessfully trying to delay the moment when she would have to see Jake.

"Hi, Sexy."

Marni spun around, retort ready, but found that Jake was speaking to Kate instead of her. Embarrassed, she started to turn away, but he spotted her.

"How are things at the bank?"

"Tiring," Kate jumped in. "Very tiring. She could barely leave the house tonight. I think it was a bank emergency. Go figure."

Marni blushed. Darn Kate, she was trying to put her on the spot, and it was working. "I feel better now, really."

"Must have been a lot of banking emergencies this week. You've been working a lot of late hours," Jake said. He was wearing a navy-blue western shirt and a pair of black form-fitting jeans. A black leather belt hugged his waist and a large silver buckle winked in the sunlight.

"Something like that," Marni mumbled and went to unload her horse from the trailer.

Twister scooted out backwards and she tied him to the side of the rig. She took off his shipping boots and tossed them into the back of the trailer. After rummaging around in the back of the truck, she found a brush to clean him up with.

"Miss me?"

Jake's silky voice came out close to her ear. He'd crept up on her again. This time Marni wished for Ben's shotgun. "Why would I miss you when I've been trying to avoid you all week?" She knew she'd just blown her story, but she didn't care. The man was maddening. *And sexier than sin one day before confession.*

"Sally says hi, by the way."

"You knew! You knew all along I've been avoiding you like a bad case of ringworm and you still won't give up."

"You won't shake me so easily. I like to win, Marni." Jake tipped his cowboy hat at her and ambled away.

Win what? she wondered. She watched him retreat like he had that day at the bank. She shook her head, refusing to stare. He was *not* that cute. *Yeah right.*

Sighing, she continued to brush Twister. The gelding preened under the attention and soon she found a rhythm that allowed her to think. Jake confused her more than any man she'd ever known. He infuriated and tantalized her. True, he was charming, but he didn't waste much of that charm on her.

Then, when he'd kissed her—almost kissed her—he'd been so tender, his touch so gentle. She expected a real kiss would sweep her away, since she couldn't stop thinking about the one that hadn't happened.

A snort from Twister pulled Marni out of those dangerous thoughts. She soon had him saddled with a loose girth, so he would be comfortable while he waited. She walked over to the entry booth to check in. Doing something practical was so much easier than trying to figure out Jake's complexities.

"Hey, Trish, you got my entries?" she asked the gray-haired whip of a show secretary.

"Sure, Marni." Trish flipped through her assorted sheets of paper. "Here you are, first in after the last drag."

Marni groaned. "First in *again*?"

"I never did understand why you hate being the top horse; most riders prefer it."

"How am I supposed to remember the pattern when I can't follow the tracks of the horse in front of me?" Marni joked.

"Seriously, why?" Trish persisted.

"Twister is a big horse. He likes to dig into that churned-up ground. When we're first in, he has to run on top of the pen and he's not as aggressive in his turns. We lose a lot of time."

"Well, that makes sense. Good luck anyway. I'm sure you'll be in the money, like every other time."

"Now you've done it. You jinxed me! How am I supposed to run my horse with a swelled head?"

"Nice to see I'm not the only one who suffers from that problem." Jake slipped in beside her at the entry booth. "Trish, Darlin', how's my favorite girl?"

"Oh, Jake, always the charmer. Could you give Frank lessons?"

"If your husband doesn't treat you nice, you can come home with me."

Trish giggled.

Marni couldn't believe it, he'd charmed another one.

Was there a female out there, besides her, who could resist him? She tried to sidestep him and leave the booth, but he slid his arm around her waist and pulled her back up to the counter. Like when he'd touched her before, her skin tingled. She could feel flutters of excitement in the pit of her stomach as he tightened his grip.

"Now Marni here, she could teach Frank how to treat a lady right. She puts me in my place regular. Why, I wasn't half as charming last weekend before I met her."

"That's an understatement," Marni muttered under her breath.

"Do I detect a little romance going on between you two?" Trish twisted her long braid in her fingers. A speculative look crossed her face.

"No!" Marni took her voice down a decibel. "I mean, no. There's *nothing* between us."

"Marni won't take me with all my rough edges, but I'm trying to improve for her sake." Jake gave her a squeeze and smiled down at her.

That evil warthog. "Just what are you up to, Harrison?"

"I'm just letting Trish know my intentions." This time the mischief in his eyes was unmistakable. "Giving her a head start on the rodeo circuit gossip." He winked at Trish. "You better hurry and warm up your horse, Marni. I'm sure he's getting restless by the trailer." Jake pushed her toward the door.

"Hey! Hold on a minute." Marni tried to dig her boot heels into the floorboards, but she couldn't stop him from pushing her out.

"Now, now, Honey. I'll be right there, I promise. You've gone this long without me, you can wait ten more minutes."

Marni snapped her mouth shut on her protest. *What did he just say?* She was about to lecture him on what he was leading Trish to believe but saw the challenging gleam in his eyes, and instead chose to turn tail and run.

She stewed all the way back to the trailer. Maybe she should have stayed and set things right with Trish. Gossip had wings, and this was one piece of misinformation she didn't want to get around. Her and Jake? She tried to avoid being on the same farm with him. Which was difficult since he practically lived at Kate and Ben's place of late. She'd have better luck avoiding him in his own home.

This was becoming a problem for Marni. With Jake at the ranch every day, people would really start to believe they were a couple. It didn't matter that she was at the bank most of the time; it would still be taken the wrong way. She had to clean up the mess Jake had made for her. The last thing she needed was another cowboy messing with her life.

Jake knew he'd be in for it when he got back to his horse trailer. There was probably an ambush waiting for him. He shouldn't have misled Trish, but it was so much fun provoking Marni.

True, they weren't a couple. True, Marni didn't like him much, but things could change. Goodness knew the chemistry between them snapped like an electric fence. Maybe she just needed a little push to convince her. *Yeah, and maybe Bart will sprout wings and fly.*

It might be better to give Marni some breathing room after the stunt he'd just pulled. He wandered over to the exercise pen and tried to blend in.

"Don't even *think* you're going to hide from me, Cowboy!" Marni's stern warning came from overhead.

Jake shuddered as it occurred to him that he made the perfect target. Marni could easily run him down with her horse. He turned slowly and smiled up at her. "There you are, Sugar. I told you I'd be done in a few minutes." He kept his voice low and soothing.

Apparently Marni didn't see it that way. The look she shot him was murderous. "You're doing it again," she whispered fiercely.

"Doing what?" Jake assumed an innocent-sounding stage whisper.

"Making people think we're a couple." She looked around at the sea of cowboy hats. Several of them turned in her direction.

"I'm just trying to keep you from running me over with Twister."

"Don't kid yourself, you're not worth the prison time."

"I—" *Probably shouldn't argue that one with her.* "I thought you were going to warm up your horse," he recovered.

"Don't change the subject. What are you up to?"

"I'm not up to anything." He slid his hands into his pockets and rocked back on his heels. "I haven't said a word that wasn't true."

Marni snorted. "What about when you told Trish I wouldn't take you with your rough edges?"

"It's true, isn't it?"

"Or when you said you were letting her know your true intentions." Marni glared at him.

"I was." He smiled. "Doesn't mean anything is actually going on between us. Yet."

"It doesn't change the fact that what you said in the entry booth and what you said here has been totally misinterpreted."

"And it's my fault?"

"Yes. No. I don't care. Just stop it!" Marni trotted Twister past Jake into the exercise pen.

"Not a chance," he said to her retreating back. He'd get through her defenses yet.

"Hey, Harrison." Sonny's smooth drawl made Jake cringe. "What's this I hear about you and Marni? You two checkin' out the local hay barns or somethin'?"

"Just a rumor, Reid. Nothing more." Jake hated to consider the other cowboy thinking of Marni that way.

"That's a relief. She's too good for you."

"Gee Sheriff, I didn't realize she came with a rating."

"You know what I mean. Marni's not the love 'em and leave 'em type. She deserves better."

"And I suppose you would be more than willing to provide her with what she needs, huh, Sonny?"

"Better me than you," was all the other cowboy said before he left.

That thought disturbed Jake. He didn't want Marni to be the prize in a competition between him and Sonny. She was different from the other women they competed over. Special. As much as he teased her, he really liked her and wanted to get to know her better.

This realization surprised him, but he didn't have time to analyze his feelings for her at the moment. The calf-roping event ran third in this evening's line up at the Mason Jar Rodeo. Right after the bareback bronc riding and the steer wrestling. He needed to prepare for the event.

Jake had warmed-up Bart before Kate and Ben arrived; now it was time for him to limber up his throwing arm. He walked back to the horse trailer and took his rope out of its bag. He found a lone garbage can near his truck and began swinging his lasso. Part of his problem last week was he hadn't warmed up properly.

It really had nothing to do with Marni.

He released his loop.

He missed the garbage can.

Well, *almost* nothing to do with her and his vivid imagination. He growled and coiled up the lifeless lariat.

"Seems you have as much trouble with stationary objects as moving ones," Marni said from behind him. "Are you sure you want to be a calf-roper? Maybe there's some other event you'd like to try?"

He turned slowly toward her. Her hair was tousled from her ride in the exercise pen. He wanted to touch her wild curls and run his fingers through their softness. Her lips spread into a smile and he was mesmerized by the possibility of what their lush fullness would feel like against his own.

"You know, the trick to roping something is you really have to want to catch it." Jake began the slow swing of his lasso again. "And of course, the object you're roping doesn't usually want to be caught." He smiled at her. "If I were you, I'd run."

She understood his intention and took off for the safety of Ben's truck. She wasn't fast enough. Jake's loop slid gracefully over her shoulders. She spun abruptly toward him and the rope tightened around her waist, pinning her arms to her sides.

"Not funny, Harrison."

He admired his catch. She certainly beat the calves he'd been roping, hands down. "I wasn't trying to be funny." He tugged on the rope a little and she took a reluctant step forward. He could feel the blood rushing through his veins. Excitement built inside him. The thrill of the chase was replaced by the victory of the capture. "You're mine," he said in a low growl before firmly pulling her toward him.

Marni struggled to free herself from the rope. She grabbed onto the line with both hands and dug her heels into the dirt. She tried to slow her forward progress, but he had her off balance and wasn't giving up his advantage.

"Relax. This won't be so bad," he said as an idea formed in his mind. "You might even like it." He drew his lips into his most mischievous smile.

"Wh—what—" she cleared her throat. "What are you going to do to me?"

He gave the rope one more tug and she took an awkward step toward him. They stood toe-to-toe. He slipped his hand under the knot and took a firm hold of her waist. His knuckles brushed against her light cotton shirt. The heat from her body warmed his skin and set his blood on fire.

He watched resistance melt away from her as she moved into his arms. She wrapped her hands around the fist that he held the knot with and tilted her chin up to his face.

Somewhere inside his clouded brain a thought floated up that as much as Marni might deny it, she was as drawn to him as he was to her. He watched her mouth as her tongue slipped out to moisten her parted lips.

He wanted to kiss her.

But . . . There was something he had to do and it wasn't kissing Marni. His brain fought its way out of the desire-induced fog.

Something about . . . "An apology," he blurted out.

"Huh?" Awareness crept into Marni's eyes where longing had overwhelmed them. He fought back a sigh at the lost opportunity, but in time there would be other chances to kiss her. First she had to trust him.

"An apology for your release," he bartered.

"A what?" She seemed to have trouble with the concept. He hoped it was because her insides felt the same as his—as churned up as the mud after a cattle stampede. "For making cracks about my roping abilities. I think I've proven that I'm quite—skilled." He looked at the rope, then Marni, raising one eyebrow.

"That's it? I say I'm sorry and you let me go?" She dropped her hands.

"Mmm-hmm. That's it. Could you hurry up though, my class is starting soon."

He thought she would get angry, stomp on his foot, or knee him in the groin, or something. Instead she surprised him with her calm voice.

"You're right. You're very—able. I'm sorry." She sounded disappointed.

Why? Jake hoped it was about not getting kissed. He knew his own lips were feeling deprived.

"Uh, Jake? The rope?"

"Oh yeah, right." He slipped the loop open and pulled the rope over her head. Immediately, he regretted the loss of her warmth.

"Good luck today," she said awkwardly as she walked away.

"You too."

He slapped the rope against his thigh. Why couldn't he have a conversation with her that didn't leave her upset with him? He was ten times the fool for continuing to push her. But she stirred something inside him whenever she was near, and a voice that came from deep within his heart told him she would be the best prize he could ever win.

"An apology," Marni berated herself. "I'm such an idiot!"

She sat on the fender of the horse trailer beside Twister. She was grateful no one had been around to witness that scene. *No one but Jake.* He wasn't even the problem, it was her. One moment she'd been ready to throw pitchforks at the guy, the next she was throwing herself at him.

"He must think I'm insane." She doubted it was far from the truth.

Every time she thought she had Jake figured out, he made a sudden right turn. She wanted to believe his personality was inconsistent, but it was probably her perception of him that was conflicting. She had tried to fit him into the same category as Roy, but he was different. Sure, he was every bit as bold and cocky as her ex, but Jake wasn't trying to impress everyone around him, just her.

Marni stood up and brushed imaginary dust off her jeans. Twister didn't stir from his hay. "I'm glad to see my ranting doesn't stress you out, Boy."

She patted the tall gelding. He turned one eye toward her, then shoved his nose forcefully into his hay bag. "I know. Less talk, more food." She laughed.

The rodeo was well underway and she heard the first call for the calf-roping competitors. She decided to wander over to the grandstand and find Ben and Kate. They were easy to spot. *End of the pen, middle of the bleachers, like always.* She made her way through the throng of people.

A hand grabbed her elbow and a wide chest brushed up against her back. "Come to see a real man rope?"

"Hi, Sonny." She twisted out of his grasp to face him. His fingers were cool, not warm like Jake's. She smiled up into his wintry blue eyes.

"If I know you're watching me, I'll win it for you," he said.

"Um, thanks." She'd heard him use the same line on Martha Miller last week. Martha had giggled and swooned.

Marni couldn't raise the same enthusiasm toward the sheriff.

Sonny was an extremely attractive cowboy. Tall, slender, blond, and tanned, he was a walking cologne ad. He was also a slick operator. He was so smooth, he made Jake look like sandpaper. Even Roy, who had all the moves down, couldn't compare to Sonny.

"After I pick up my check, we'll celebrate." He winked and strode off confidently into the crowd.

She smiled to herself over the boldness of these cowboys. *Whoever said they were the strong, silent type never got off the chuck wagon.* There were so many peacocks on the circuit someone could start an aviary.

Marni climbed up into the bleachers and plunked herself down beside Kate.

Ben leaned over his wife and asked, "Where have you been?"

"Um, I was tied up at the trailer," Marni said casually.

Kate gave her a strange look and Marni worried she knew something.

"Calf-roping is about to start," Kate said.

So that's what the look was for. "Really?" She kept her eyes fixed on the arena and never let on she had come to see Jake compete. "I thought they were still bronc riding. Guess I'll have to watch this instead."

Marni could feel Kate looking at her, so she did the only thing a coward in her place could do. Lie. "Ooh, look, there's Sonny. Doesn't he look divine in the saddle?"

"Sure Marni, he's great." Kate shrugged her shoulders and turned back to the action.

The first rider missed his calf, but the next three made good ties. Jake was the fifth rider in. Marni's stomach clenched as she watched him put his horse in the chute. He nodded and the calf was released into the arena. It shot through the barrier line first.

Each swing of Jake's lasso tightened Marni's nerves another notch. When he loosed his line, she held her breath. The loop caught and Bart snapped the rope tight.

Marni straightened in her seat.

Jake exploded out of the saddle and ran toward the calf. He threw it to the ground and had it tied in three quick flicks of his wrist. He raised his arm to stop the timer.

He didn't get snagged by his line. Marni smiled to herself. The time would be good.

Bart stood still while Jake remounted. After the six-second delay, the announcer declared the tie legal and gave his time. It was good. Very good. He was in first place. Jake tipped his hat to the judge and left the arena.

Marni hurried to get Twister ready at the trailer. She tightened his girth, rechecked the rigging on her saddle, and put on his bridle. She climbed up onto his back and trotted over to the ring. Jake had won his class and she had stayed to watch the presentations. It was the reason she was late.

When she got to the pen, Kate was just exiting the arena.

"What's the footing on the course like?" Marni asked.

"A little shallow, but the horses ahead of me seemed to handle it all right."

Marni nodded. Kate was a good horsewoman. If she didn't think the conditions were safe, she wouldn't run her horse.

"Good luck." Kate walked Angel past Marni and Twister.

"Thanks."

The other competitors quickly completed their barrel runs. Soon it was time for Marni to enter the arena.

She trotted Twister through the chute and was at a full gallop before she reached the end. She sat deep in the saddle at the first barrel and signaled him to slow for his turn. The gelding started to slide.

He scrambled for a hold and she tried to balance him with the reins. She could feel him overcompensating, his feet slipping out from underneath him. The feeling of falling seemed to slow the action. The impact came before she could react.

Marni was jerked partially out of the saddle when Twister fell. She landed flat on her back with her left leg pinned under the horse. Her lungs burned to take in air, but her throat seemed closed.

Twister rolled off her leg and stood. Before she could see if he was okay, a wide pair of shoulders and a concerned face blocked her view. *Jake.* She struggled to sit up, anything to relieve the pressure in her chest and let her breathe.

He gently pressed her back into the dirt. "Easy, Marni, you've had the wind knocked out of you. Try to relax."

From behind him, she heard people talking. Someone said, "Twister's hurt."

Someone else said, "Thank goodness he fell away from the barrel."

Marni felt hot tears coursing down her cheeks. She closed her eyes and struggled to relax. The air came rushing back into her lungs. "Twister," she gasped.

Jake looked over his shoulder and then back at her. "Nothing's broken; other than that I can't tell."

She found that she could breathe easier, but her heart was threatening to burst over concern for her horse. She struggled against the firm grip that held her down. "Let me see!"

Jake released her shoulders and gave her his hand to help her up. When she was on her feet, he stepped out of her way. She was already stiffening up and would be sore tomorrow, but her legs would hold her for now.

The big bay gelding stood quietly while Ben took off his splint boot. He felt the horse's leg and put it down.

Marni could see the problem before Ben said anything. "It's a bowed tendon." Her voice cracked.

Her first thought was one of relief. *He'll heal.* But a selfish part of her was heavy with the knowledge the season was over for her and she wouldn't win the championship. All her hard work for nothing. It would be at least another year before her dream could come true and she could finally put her father's wish to rest.

Chapter Five

Jake tapped on Ben and Kate's door. It was still raining and he was thankful for the porch roof over his head.

Again the scenario of Marni falling raced through his mind. He'd thought for sure his heart had stopped as he'd watched her hit the ground. Then everything had sped up as he'd vaulted the arena fence and run to the spot where she lay. His heart hadn't started beating again until he'd realized she was okay. At that moment he had understood that Marni meant more to him than a one-night stand or a casual acquaintance.

He heard feet padding toward the entrance and stepped back as the door swung open. A blast of warm dry air surrounded him.

"Jake," Kate said. "Didn't expect to see you this evening."

"Hi, Kate. I was looking for Marni. Is she here? She didn't answer her door."

"She's in the living room with Ben." Kate motioned Jake

into the front hall. "Why don't you take off your boots and sit a spell?"

"Thanks." He hung his jacket and cowboy hat on a coat peg. The smell of shampoo wafted through the air when he lifted his hat off his head and ran his fingers through his damp hair.

"Looks like you got yourself all slicked up to come over here." Kate tapped a button on his western shirt. "Should I be flattered?"

"Kate, I've got to confess something to you." Jake hung his head in mock guilt. "There's someone else."

"What?" Kate pretended to be horrified. "I thought I was your woman."

"You are, but I was hoping to take Marni out for a drink."

"Oh . . . Marni. That's okay then. She's practically one of my own. Babysat her when she was a young 'un. As long as you keep it in the family."

Jake laughed. "And just what are you accusing me of, woman?"

"Nothing." Kate smiled. "Guess you better go ask her before she gets a better offer. Go on in and I'll get you a cup of coffee."

Jake walked into the cozy living room. Light from the elk-horn chandelier illuminated the place. His eyes drifted to the leather chair where Marni was curled up with a mug in her small hands.

"Evenin'," he said as he stepped through the doorway. "Care if I join you?"

Marni's eyes met Jake's and she smiled. For the first time her smile looked completely genuine, and he wondered at that. She looked small and meek, like someone had beaten the spirit out of her.

He took the matching chair beside hers.

"What brings you out tonight, Jake?" Ben asked. "Can't paint fence posts in the rain and dark."

"Well, darn it." Jake made to get out of his chair. "I guess I'll just have to go on home then."

Ben laughed and waved him back down.

"So if you're not here to work, then what are the fancy duds for?" Marni asked.

"I thought I might find an unsuspecting cowgirl to dance with."

"Here?" Marni looked at him funny.

"No, at the Chug and Chew Bar and Grill."

"Oh, well . . . good luck then." She looked disappointed. "When are you going?"

"As soon as my date gets herself together and tells me she's ready to leave."

Realization dawned across Marni's face. "Me? I don't think so, Jake. I'm still sore from yesterday. Besides, I don't think I could stand the sympathy."

"Then I promise not to give you any."

She laughed at that. "I know better than to expect it from you. I meant from the other riders. I'm sure some of them will be there."

"Well, I think you should go." Kate stood in the doorway holding Jake's coffee mug. She walked to his chair and handed it to him, then sat down next to her husband on the couch. "Dancing will work some of the kinks out of your stiff muscles."

"Do you have anything to say about this?" Marni turned to Ben. "Since my opinion doesn't count in this household."

"When you pay full room and board for yourself and Twister, you can have an opinion," he answered.

"I try to pay rent. You two won't let me."

"Beside the point." Ben winked at Jake, then looked at Marni. "Hurry up and get changed. Your date's waiting."

Marni glanced at Jake and he wiggled his eyebrows at her. She groaned and hauled herself out of her chair. "Don't think I'm getting all dolled up for you," she threw back at him as she left the room.

Jake smiled, glad to see some of her spirit back.

"So why do I get the feeling you're interested in more than a dancing partner?" Kate asked him after they heard the front door shut.

"The truth is I have a proposal for Marni," Jake answered.

"Ooooh, he's going to propose!"

"A little fast isn't it, Jake?" Ben asked. "Marni hardly knows you. I'm all for it, but she'll put up a fight, for sure. Need my shotgun?"

"A *business* proposal! I meant a business proposal." Jake backpedaled. "I was going to ask her if she wants to use one of my horses. I won't propose anything. I promise." He swiped at an imaginary bead of sweat on his forehead and sunk lower into his chair.

"Darn, I thought we were going to have us a wedding." Kate pretended to pout. "Maybe you better get your shotgun, Ben. We'll need to use it on both of them."

Jake listened to Kate and Ben speculate about his marriage to Marni. Normally, the mere mention of the big 'M' would send him running for the door. He fantasized about a life with her. They would have kids, maybe two or three. He could picture her swollen pregnant belly and the pretty floral maternity dresses she would wear. He really liked what he was imagining. Until he got to the part where she clobbered him with a frying pan for touching her.

"Hey." Ben waved a beefy paw under Jake's nose. "You with us, Cowboy? When are you going to ask Marni about the horse?"

Jake's attention snapped back from where it had been. "Tonight, I think. At the bar. You know her better. Will she say yes?"

"I can't see her passing up the opportunity," Kate interjected. "Even if you are the booby prize that goes along with it."

"Hey! I'm not that bad."

"Depends on who you ask," Ben said.

They heard the front door open. "I'm ready." Marni's voice floated in from the hallway.

"Guess that's my cue to leave." Jake got out of his chair. "See you both later."

He walked into the front entrance. Marni was playing with the buttons on her navy blue sweater. A white T-shirt peeked through the opening at the top. She was by far the sexiest woman he had ever seen.

Jake whistled through clenched teeth. "Aren't you a cowboy's wish in tight jeans."

"A compliment?" Marni teased. "Isn't that something you give other people?"

"What do you mean?" Jake asked as he pulled on his roper boots.

"Since I met you I've been the lucky receiver of all your insults. Tonight you're being nice to me. How come?"

"Maybe I'm not being nice." He straightened as he put his hat on his head. "Maybe I'm just stating the obvious."

"Because you're a man who believes in scientific fact?"

"Darn right." Jake shrugged on his jacket and led her out the door.

They got in his truck; he started it and drove down the

long lane to the highway. He was proud of himself for getting Marni away from the farm so easily. "Want to listen to some music?" he asked, reaching for the tuning knob.

"I'll get it," she blurted out and took control of the radio.

By the careful way she avoided his arm, he suspected she was trying to keep from touching him. Jake smiled and put his hand back on the steering wheel. He'd let her get away with it for now, but they were going to be spending a lot of time together. She couldn't avoid him forever.

Most of the drive to the Chug and Chew passed in friendly silence. The parking lot was full when Jake pulled in. Amazingly, he found a spot near the entrance and they got out.

Jake opened the bar door for Marni. Music, laughter, voices, and smoke surrounded them.

"Busy place," she remarked.

"No kidding. Let's find a booth near the bar and away from the dance floor. It won't be so loud there."

He took advantage of the opportunity to seize her hand and navigate through the crowd. Her hand was small and warm in his grasp, and he had to let it go too soon. He spotted a booth a couple were vacating and grabbed it.

So many bodies pressed together made the Chug and Chew a warm place, and Marni took off her sweater before she sat down. She was wearing a plain white T-shirt that fit her curves as snugly as her jeans did. Jake knew she hadn't done anything special to her appearance, but he thought she looked great anyway.

Face it, Harrison, you'd think she looked great in a burlap sack . . . or less. Jake shook himself out of his wayward thoughts. Once his mind traveled down that path he'd have a hard time reining it back, and he had other business with Marni tonight.

"Do you want something to drink?" he asked her.

"Sure. Make it a beer. Earl doesn't do fancy very well."

Jake smiled. "So you've been here before."

"Yeah, once or twice."

Marni watched him thread his way to the bar. He was one fine-looking cowboy, and tonight he was all hers.

Whoa, girl! Where did that come from? She knew how dangerous it would be to get involved with Jake. Sure, he had been the first one to get to her when she fell with Twister, and he had been nice to her for a whole twenty-four hours. Those were good enough reasons to give him a chance, but she needed to be careful of whom she trusted her heart to, and Jake was still a cowboy. A charming one too, and that meant she had no business longing for him. His love would be like Roy's: it was the kind meant for sharing . . . with more than one woman.

Still, it didn't mean they couldn't be friends. Sooner or later she'd become immune to the crazy attraction. After all, it was just lust. *Wasn't it?*

Her analysis of Jake was interrupted when Sonny slid in the booth across from her.

"Howdy, Beautiful." The compliment rolled too smoothly off his tongue. "Please tell me you're here to see me and not with that loser Harrison."

"Sorry to disappoint you, but I came with Jake." Marni thought she saw a look of distaste cross Sonny's face, but it was gone before she was sure.

"Does that mean the rumors are true? You two have a thing going?" He made the concept sound repulsive.

"No! Of course not. We're just friends."

The sheriff smiled and visibly relaxed. "Good, because

he's been snuggling up to Carol-Anne since he went over to the bar." Sonny pointed his thumb in their direction.

Marni spotted them immediately. Carol-Anne was walking her fingers down Jake's shirtfront to his belt buckle. She laughed at something he said and tossed her long brown locks playfully. Marni felt bitterness and jealousy take hold of her. It was happening again.

No. It's not. This isn't the same. You just said that you and Jake are only friends. The thought didn't reassure her.

"They used to have a thing a few years back when Jake was calf-roping champion on the rodeo circuit."

"Huh?" Marni was so focused on the couple she had forgotten there was someone else at the table.

"Yeah, Carol-Anne's a real classic. She's with you when you're winning, all lovey and smiles, but when the checks stop coming in, she drops you like a hot rock. They kinda suit each other, don't you think?"

"What do you mean?"

"Well, Jake's only interested in the challenge of winning a woman over. Once he has her, the thrill is gone." Sonny eyed her meaningfully. "You're too good for a guy like him."

"There's nothing between us. Jake just helps Ben out at the farm. I hardly ever see him."

"I know, you told me." He winked at her. "I was just making sure. I've got to go water the race horse, Darlin'. Promise you'll save me a dance for later." He tipped his hat and weaved unsteadily through the crowd.

Sonny must be drunk. His pick-up lines are getting worse.

Marni's gaze drifted again across the smoky room to Jake and Carol-Anne. They were still pressed tightly together. She was whispering something in his ear and he was shaking his head.

This was more than Marni could take. "Darn it, Jake, you're making me look like a fool," she whispered fiercely. "If you think you can leave me here while you go chasing rodeo queens, you have another thing coming."

She grabbed her sweater and pushed through the bodies that blocked the path to the door. *I'll find my own way home.*

She was making good progress until Trish and Frank stopped her.

"Honey," Trish said. "Didn't expect to see you here tonight. How's your horse doing?"

Marni wanted to pretend she didn't hear her and make a run for the door, but that would be rude. Besides, Kate would give her a ride home whether she called now or five minutes from now. The hard part would be avoiding Jake until Kate got to the bar.

Jake saw Marni leave the booth and work her way to the exit. He wanted to holler at her, but knew she wouldn't stop. Instead, he grabbed the two beers the bartender had left for him and pulled his arm out of Carol-Anne's grip.

"Nice talking to you, Honey, but I have to go. My date's trying to leave without me." He forced his way through the crowd, glad to have a reason to get away from the rodeo queen.

He had once thought Carol-Anne was the best catch on the circuit. He'd been wrong. When she left him, she taught him a hard lesson: people are only interested in what you can give them. Though he didn't believe it of everyone he knew, it was true of the women he had dated.

They always wanted something from him. Jennifer had

wanted him for his ranch. Isabella had wanted a cowboy. And Tracy had only wanted—well, let's just say there was only so much a man could give.

Now Carol-Anne wanted him back, and he couldn't imagine why. She'd already spent half his savings and the other half was buried into the ranch. The only other possible reason could be Marni. Carol-Anne might not want him, but she probably wouldn't let another woman have him either. She had always been a little jealous.

Jake reached Marni's side before she could get past Trish and her husband Frank. He seized her wrist and pulled her close to his chest as she tried to walk away from them.

"Where do you think you're going?" he asked. "I haven't finished my beer yet." He waved their two full bottles under her nose.

Marni tried to pull her wrist out of his grip. "Oh, you're finished all right. Your horse never even made it out of the chute."

"You're mad about Carol-Anne. Sit down, have a drink with me, and I'll explain."

He tugged her back to their booth and placed their beers on the table. Then he slid in beside her so she couldn't escape.

"Jake, leave me alone," she huffed. "I just want to go home. I don't know what I'm doing here with you anyway."

"You're still here, and since you are . . ." He slid her beer toward her as a peace offering.

"Fine." She took the bottle. "I'll sit and have a lousy beer, but then I'm leaving."

He stared at her in silence as she took a swallow. A storm raged in her eyes as she glared at him over her drink and her cheeks were flushed. She was as riled as a rank bronc.

He chuckled. She was trying to ignore him, but he knew how to get a reaction out of her. There was no way she would sit there in silence all night.

"What are you thinking?" Marni asked. She shifted in her seat away from him.

He let his leg brush against hers. She tried to move away, but there was nowhere for her to go. She was already pressed against the side of the booth. Her gaze broke away from his.

"I'm not him, you know."

"What are you talking about?"

"Your ex-boyfriend, or fiancé, or whoever he was. I'm not the cowboy who broke your heart."

"I know that, it's just . . ."

Jake encouraged her with a gentle smile.

"I caught Roy in a hotel room with another woman. I've been gun-shy ever since. Seeing Carol-Anne throw herself at you just reminded me I have to be careful who I trust."

"Well, first I'd like to say that Roy is a fool, and second I want to explain about Carol-Anne."

"Your past exploits don't interest me, Jake."

"How about my current ones?"

"I don't care about them either. What you do in your free time is your business."

"Jealous?" he whispered in her ear. He sat back to watch her reaction.

She stared at his chest when she answered him. "No." She swallowed. "Why would you think I was jealous?"

"Because it would give me a reason to be. What was Sonny doing over here?"

"Telling me about you and Carol-Anne."

"So if you knew she used to be my girlfriend why did you run?"

Marni looked uncomfortable. "He said other stuff too."

Jake nodded. He didn't like where this was heading, but if he told Marni Sonny was probably just jealous he would look defensive. At least he could set things straight about Carol-Anne. "Not that it matters, but I didn't interest her for long. She's only attracted to shiny things and money. It didn't take her long to go through mine."

"She seemed pretty interested back there." Marni hitched her thumb at the bar where the rodeo queen was now snuggling up to Sonny.

"It won't last. There'll always be someone who brings home a bigger check than I do. I just hope that when she finds what she's looking for she isn't disappointed." Jake wondered if Marni was the same type of girl—always more interested in what a man could give her than in the man himself. He was about to give her a real good reason to like him. Could she be different? Would he ever find a woman who would see more than his material qualities?

"I'm sorry." Marni placed her hand on his sleeve. "I thought you wanted to be with her and I was in the way. I overreacted."

Marni's nearness undid all his self-control. "Don't apologize yet." He'd been wondering so long what her lips would feel like he couldn't wait another second. He leaned forward to kiss her.

"Jake—"

"Hold that thought." He dipped his head down to touch her full lips. They tasted as good as lemonade on a hot summer's day and felt as soft as the petals of a daisy. Her silence was inviting, and he slid his hand behind her neck to cradle her head. Chestnut curls licked at his wrist.

She leaned into his touch. He closed his eyes as he nibbled on her bottom lip. The moan that fled her throat didn't escape his attention.

He sighed and took deeper possession of her mouth. He had craved this woman since first seeing her. To be able to finally hold her was a greater reward than he had expected. She was hot and sweet in his arms, and he wanted to keep kissing her except—

Except for the insistent coughing behind him.

Jake broke away from Marni and glared angrily at the source of the noise.

"Sir?" The waiter's voice cracked and Jake wondered if he was old enough to be here. "That guy over there," he pointed in the direction of the bar, "wanted you to have these."

"And it couldn't wait?" Jake asked. He tried to spot the instigator of the interruption.

"He insisted I deliver them immediately." The waiter placed two beer bottles on the table. "He said it couldn't wait."

Jake finally found the culprit. Sonny smirked, tipped his hat, and then returned to the bar and Carol-Anne's attention.

Jake turned back to Marni, but her mood had already changed; she looked embarrassed and ruffled.

"Drink your beer, Marni," Jake said moodily. "It's getting warm."

He decided that giving her some space was probably safer than risking a black eye, so he moved to the other side of the table.

The silence became uncomfortable. "I know you think I conned you into a date, but I didn't bring you here to dance," he finally said.

"You mean we aren't dancing?" she teased.

He was glad she was beginning to relax around him. "No, 'fraid not. I can teach you all about dancing later. First I have something I want to ask you."

"I don't have any terrible vices and I don't like the color pink."

Jake laughed at her quick retort. "Okay, we can go dance now."

"What do you really want to ask me?"

"Oh, that. Well, since you don't have a horse to ride, I was wondering if you want to use one of mine." He held up his hand as she started to object. "The more exposure my horses get, the better my chances of selling them. You'll be doing me a favor."

"I don't know what to say." She seemed truly surprised by his offer.

"How about yes," Jake said. "We can hash out the details later."

Conflicting emotions raced across her face. She wanted to say yes, as far as Jake could tell. "There's no catch," he added.

"Yes!" she blurted out, then laughed. "I can't believe this. I thought my barrel-racing season was over. You have no idea what this means to me!"

"I think I can guess."

"Do you have a specific horse in mind?"

"Lady," he smiled at her before continuing, "do I have a horse for you. She isn't as tall as Twister, but she's quick on her feet and spunky, just like you."

"Obviously you haven't seen me dance, otherwise you'd realize that I'm not as quick on my feet as my horse is on his," Marni responded.

"I think I can fix that." Jake got up and pulled her out of the booth. "I'm almost as good at dancing as I am at—"

"I don't think I want to hear this," Marni interrupted.

"Roping. I was going to say roping. Get your mind out of the gutter, Woman." Jake tugged her onto the dance floor. "If you're not careful someone might take your comments the wrong way." He looped an arm around her waist and pulled her against him.

"Like you?" Marni teased.

"Absolutely." He took her hand and started to move. "First lesson is, I lead."

"Okay, Mr. Murray."

"I prefer Arthur." He tightened his grip around her waist. "Lesson number two is, relax and trust me."

The command made Marni stiffen in his arms. He spun with her in a circle and again took the rhythm of the two-step so she was forced to loosen up and follow his lead.

"Better," Jake whispered in her ear.

They began to move together, his steps mirrored by hers. He could feel her heart hammering against his chest. She tipped her head back and smiled at him. He knew he had her again.

"Told you I could teach you how to dance."

"It's not the first time I've done this, you know. I just don't do it very often and I forget how in between."

"I promise you won't forget this time." He spun her again and leaned her back over his arm in a quick dip.

"Pretty sure of yourself, aren't you?"

He swung her back up. "Confident in my style, actually. I haven't had any complaints yet."

"There's always a first time."

"No way, I offer a guarantee."

"Money back?" she asked with a mischievous gleam in her eye.

"No, a guarantee of service. You can keep coming back until I get it right."

"Oh." She blushed, not missing his meaning. "I'm getting a little warm; maybe I should sit down."

"I'm not finished with you yet, Marni." Jake felt a tap on his shoulder.

"Mind if we cut in?" Sonny hauled Carol-Anne up beside him.

Smooth move, Sheriff, but I don't think so. Jake looked at Marni and tightened his grip possessively around her. If she wanted to dance with Sonny, she was going to have to say so herself, because he sure as heck wasn't giving her up.

She didn't say anything, so Jake answered for her. "Marni's still sore from her fall yesterday. She was just asking me if she could sit down, but I think I'll take her home." He turned to look at her. "If that's okay with you."

"Come on, Sugar," Carol-Anne urged. "It's only one dance."

Marni yawned and put a hand to her back. "I really think I should go home. I'll be paying for this tomorrow."

Jake was pleased by her response, even though he was pretty sure it had more to do with Carol-Anne than not wanting to dance with the sheriff.

"Maybe some other time." Sonny smiled at her. "You still owe me a dance." He pulled Carol-Anne into his embrace and she giggled as they two-stepped across the floor.

Jake took Marni back to the booth to retrieve her sweater and his jacket. "I really had better get you home. You have a big day ahead."

"What do you mean? I don't work until Monday."

"No, but you'll be at my place bright and early tomorrow to try out my horse." He gave her her sweater. "Of course, you could come home with me. I'll make you breakfast in the morning and we could start earlier."

She blanched. "I don't eat breakfast," she mumbled and quickly darted out of the bar.

Chapter Six

Marni stood at Jake's front door. She raised her hand to knock and lowered it again. "What am I doing here?" she muttered to herself.

That morning she had called her father and told him what had happened. He had been anxious about her fall and was relieved to hear that she was fine and Twister would eventually recover. He wasn't as disappointed about her losing a chance at the championship as she'd expected. He was downright thrilled to hear about Jake's offer.

Marni would be excited too, if she weren't so anxious about spending time with Jake. True, she wanted a chance at the championship buckle. She'd be a fool not to accept his generous offer, but it would mean letting him into her life. Last night proved how dangerous that would be. She never should have allowed him to kiss her, but she'd lost control of her common sense when his lips touched hers. Even the interruption of the waiter hadn't really cooled her ardor.

She couldn't hold on to her defenses with Jake no matter

what he did, and that meant she couldn't keep her distance from him either. But struggling over what she should do about the cowboy wouldn't get her a buckle. She held her breath and rapped her knuckles against his door.

"I was wondering if you were ever going to knock," Jake said from behind her. He was standing on the bottom porch step grinning at her. "Mind telling me why you were staring at my door for the last five minutes?"

She turned around and tried to hide her embarrassment at being caught. "Looking for paint chips?"

"Nope. I painted it last month. Want to try again?"

"I was wondering if I should look for you in the barn." The excuse sounded flat, but she couldn't come up with anything else. She wasn't about to tell him she was afraid to knock on his door because his kisses made her dizzy. She was afraid she wouldn't be able to keep her hands off him.

"Well, you found me. Come to the barn. I want you to meet Chance."

Jake was definitely a morning person. And an irresistible one too. Dressed in tight denim, he looked like he'd just stepped out of a jeans ad.

"Your horse's name is Chance?" Marni asked, dragging her attention away from the cowboy's attire and back to the reason she was at his ranch.

"No, *your* horse's name is Chance." He led her through the barn to a small corral in the back.

The animal inside the pen whinnied at them and approached the fence. She was chestnut in color with a white star in the middle of her forehead. She tossed her head up and down in greeting and her forelock bounced messily around her ears.

"This is Chance." Jake motioned toward the mare. "She's a four-year-old heartbreaker."

Marni reached out her hand to pet the horse. Chance nuzzled it looking for food. When she didn't find any, she returned her attention to Jake and gave him a shove with her nose.

"I can see your horses aren't spoiled." Marni laughed. "If you don't feed this one soon, she'll drop dead of starvation."

Chance snorted at them and turned her back. She walked further into the corral to scrounge for leftover hay.

"She'd certainly like you to believe that," Jake said. "If I let her eat everything she wanted, she wouldn't be able to fit through the barn door."

"Sounds like Twister's soul mate," Marni joked.

"How's he doing?"

"The vet was out to see him again this morning. There's not much I can do except give him lots of stall rest and a considerable amount of time off."

Jake nodded. "I'm sure with your gentle touch to nurse him he'll be fine." He looked back at the mare. "Until then you have Chance to keep you occupied. So, do you want to try her out?"

Marni couldn't contain her grin. "Do horses like carrots? Of course I do! I didn't come here for your company."

"No, but if you would let me try I'm sure my company would keep you coming back." He turned and disappeared into the barn to retrieve the riding tack.

She was left blushing at Jake's comment; he made her feel so uncertain about him. Sometimes he was bold, pushy, and the perfect model of an arrogant rodeo cowboy. Then there were times, like now, when he was generous and kind beyond her expectations. Roy would have used Twister's injury against her. Told her it was proof she shouldn't be barrel racing. Jake seemed to understand her drive to be successful on the circuit, even when he didn't know her other reasons. Like her desire to make her father proud and the need to prove she could do it.

"Jake?" she asked hesitantly as he made his way back from the barn with a saddle on one hip and an armload of equipment. "Why are you being so nice to me?"

He looked surprised by her question. "Because you're a nice person," he said. He turned away from her to put the tack and brushes down and went inside the corral. He whistled to Chance and she trotted over to him. She put down her head while he slid her halter on and stood patiently while he tied her to the fence.

Marni mulled over his answer. It was logical enough, except for the fact that she wasn't really nice to Jake. When she wasn't kissing him, or dancing with him, she was insulting him and calling him an egotistical pervert.

"I'm *not* nice to you," she blurted out before she could check the thought.

"It's okay, Marni. I like you despite yourself," he teased.

I could say the same thing about you, Cowboy. "I just can't understand why you want to do this for me."

He shrugged. "Maybe one day you'll return the favor."

Jake returned to the horse and put the saddle pad on her back before he swung the saddle up and over.

Marni liked the way he moved. His actions were so fluid. His muscles tightened and stretched as he adjusted the equipment. She berated herself for not helping him while she continued to watch.

He put the bridle on the willing mare and adjusted the throatlatch. "She hasn't been ridden in weeks," he said to Marni. "Maybe I should get on her first?"

"Would I pass up the opportunity to see you tossed off a horse?" she ribbed.

"As long as you promise to kiss better any injuries I get, I'm game." He threw himself easily onto Chance's back and urged her into a walk.

Marni's reply froze in her throat as she watched the graceful exchange between horse and cowboy. They moved together as one: the horse responding to the rider.

The moment was broken when Jake pushed the mare into a jog. She snorted and threw her head before she raced off into a gleeful spree of bucks. Chance was clearly enjoying the ride she was giving Jake. Her ears were perked forward and she bounced off the ground like a rubber ball.

"Hey, hey, hey," he admonished the little mare. "There's someone on your back up here!" Despite the scolding, he rode through her spree, and when she stopped bucking he slowed her into an easy lope.

"I hope her joyriding doesn't frighten you off. She's so happy to be ridden she can't contain herself." He stopped the horse in front of her.

"Only makes her interesting and a bit of a challenge." Marni climbed over the fence rails and took the reins while Jake dismounted. "You can't expect me to back down easily."

"No." He looked at her seriously. "I don't expect many things send you running scared." A challenge of his own glimmered in the deep blue depths of his eyes.

Run! a voice screamed inside her head. *If you take him by surprise he might not catch you before you reach your truck.* She steadied her nerves. "Depends on the challenge," she said boldly.

Jake handed her the reins and she climbed up in the

saddle. He adjusted the stirrups for her while she held Chance steady. "Ready?" he asked.

Marni nodded and sent the mare into a jog. She was immediately lost in the experience. Chance felt so right underneath her. It was like an instant bond had formed between her and the animal. When Marni moved the mare up into a lope she knew she was falling in love. Even Twister, a horse she'd had for five years, didn't feel so connected to her when she rode him.

This is the horse. Marni knew she could ride a hundred other horses and never find one like Chance.

"I'm guessing by the smile on your face that you like her."

"Yes. Are you sure you want to lend her to me? I might never give her back."

"I'm willing to take my chances. If you still like her as much by the end of the season you can have the first bid to buy her."

"Are you serious?" This was the best offer Marni had heard in a long time. "What's the catch?"

"I told you last night there wasn't one, unless you count putting up with me. I'll be at the farm all day and most of the night. Could get ugly."

"Honey, you're already ugly," Marni retorted playfully. "It couldn't get worse."

"Wait till you get off your horse," he threatened. "I'll get even."

Marni didn't doubt it. The problem was she'd probably like Jake's form of retribution, and she couldn't trust herself to say no.

Hot sun and noxious fumes fired Jake's skin and his lungs as he painted the fence. The slap of the brush against the wood took up a rhythm and his mind wandered. He'd hardly seen Marni since he'd trailered Chance over to Kate and Ben's farm a week and a half ago. But in his mind he saw her every day.

Every hour.

Every minute.

He saw her slender hands and long fingers. He felt them on his skin. When he was dreaming. When he was awake. He saw her velvety lips. Tasted their sweetness and woke to find she wasn't there at all. He got lost in her eyes. Drowned in their depths, then surfaced on her smile.

He was losing his mind. *What red-blooded cowboy waxes poetic over a woman?* A horse? Yes. A prime piece of land? Yes. Even his dog. But a woman?

The thing was, Marni was proving harder to catch than a wild filly. Every time he had her cornered she ducked away from him and hid. At the rate he was going he might get to kiss her again by Christmas under the mistletoe, with Ben and Kate holding her in place.

Jake sighed and sat back on his heels. Ever muscle in his body ached, some of them screamed. He wore an open shirt to protect his back from the sun, but it seemed instead to hold the searing heat against his skin.

A rivulet of sweat rolled off one temple and he wiped it away with the back of his wrist. The action jarred a drop of white paint from the brush and it fell on his cheek. "Gall-darn-it!" he cursed and smeared it from his face with the other hand.

"You paintin' the fence or yourself?" Marni stood ten feet away, holding a glass of lemonade and looking for all the world like an oasis.

Jake thought he was hallucinating, but she came closer and pressed the cold drink into his empty hand. "Thanks," he said. He stood staring at the rapidly melting ice in his glass and tried not to think too hard about the woman standing in front of him.

"It's lemonade," she said. "I didn't poison it or anything, Girl Scout's honor." She held up her hand and crossed her fingers.

"That's not the scouts salute."

"Okay, so I never was a Girl Scout. But the lemonade's safe; Kate made it."

Jake set down his paintbrush. "Well, in that case . . ." He took a long swallow. The liquid soothed his parched throat. He ran the dewy glass across his forehead. The cool wetness soothed his heated brow.

Marni watched him intently. She was wearing a loose gray T-shirt with a tear near her right hip. He stared at the hole with barely tamed fasination.

Don't go there, Cowboy.

His eyes wandered to the pair of shorts she had on. They were cut-offs from an old, well-worn pair of jeans. A few long threads hung down her thighs.

He licked his lips. They tasted tangy and sweet from the lemonade. She rocked one ankle back and forth nervously, noticing his attention.

Jake's gaze was drawn up her slender legs. It occurred to him this was the first time he had seen them bare before. Her skin was smooth and tanned, her calves curved gracefully from the muscles underneath.

He moved his gaze slowly up to her eyes. She didn't turn away. She didn't even breathe. No insult rolled off her tongue. Not a word. She seemed to be stopped in time. Captured within a moment.

He carefully set his glass on the fence post, never breaking eye contact.

"Marni."

The word crackled into the silence.

Oh no, oh no, oh no, she thought. *What do I do?*

Jake looked more tempting than ice cream on a hot day. She let her gaze drop to his chest. His shirt was unbuttoned and each breath he took gave her a glimpse of his torso. His muscles were hard. Chiseled. Shaped by years of demanding work on the ranch. Her eyes wandered up to his shoulders, wide and strong, like she had noticed before. They were the opposite of his narrow hips.

He took a step toward her. Somewhere in the back of her mind a voice reminded her she shouldn't be here. *This is Jake.* She was sure he wasn't interested in more than a quick tumble between the sheets.

Jake wasn't professing his undying love and devotion like Roy had. He didn't want to own her or control her. He only wanted to have a little fun. Marni knew it would be good, but she wasn't so sure she'd be able to let go when it was over.

Still . . . she couldn't overcome her desire for Jake with common sense. She moved into his embrace as if he had pulled her there and he pressed his lips to hers.

She was overwhelmed by his passion. She was sure his heat would burn her up and leave only ashes. Marni closed her eyes, held his face between her palms, and took control of the kiss.

He tasted like lemonade and leather. It was an intoxicating combination that was pure Jake. She ran her hands down his arms and then back up. She pulled away and looked into his face, her own longing reflected in his eyes.

Jake's desire seared her, but it was something else that held her gaze. Something beneath the lust that looked like yearning, a tenderness she chose to ignore. He seemed to be staring straight into her soul and breaking past her defenses. But what would he do with what he found there? She pushed the thought away. There was no sense pretending Jake was someone he could never be.

She tried to shake herself out of the spell of passion he had woven around her. She would not be swept away by desire again. Roy used her attraction to him to control her. She had no reason to believe Jake would do the same thing, but also she didn't think he wanted more than a quick roll in the hay. A kiss on the cheek and a "Thank you, Ma'am" and he'd ride off into the sunset. Alone. Just like a true cowboy.

Marni saw a cloud of dust sweep down the long driveway. Reason and awareness flooded back into her brain. It had to be Kate coming back from the feed store. She pushed at Jake's chest and untangled herself from his embrace. What had she been thinking?

"What's wrong?" Jake's confusion was evident in his face. He took a step toward her, ready to capture her again.

Marni stumbled back a few more paces, shaking her head. Embarrassment coursed through her where desire had flowed freely moments before. A new heat burned her cheeks. "Kate—" she started to say.

"Knows we're adults and has enough sense not to meddle with our relationship."

"No." Marni raised her palm. "Stop. There's no relationship. *Nothing* is going on between us."

He didn't say anything. But he stood back and waited for her explanation.

"I'm sorry," Marni said. "I shouldn't have kissed you. We're supposed to be partners, friends at best. I . . ." She shook her head again. "I'm not ready for this. I'm sorry."

She clenched her fists at her sides, turned on her heel, and quickly walked back to the barn to help Kate unload the truck. She could feel Jake's gaze burning a hole through her back. If he packed up his horse and never spoke to her again she couldn't blame him.

What a stupid thing to do! Where was my head? She recalled what had just happened and shivered. She hadn't been thinking at all. One look from Jake and logic had fled her mind. Her brain could only process the sensations in her nerve endings—intense electric surges that overloaded any other thought.

I'm in serious trouble. She walked into the cool, dimly-lit barn. Being near Jake and staying uninvolved with him was proving impossible. Yet the thought of tangling with another cowboy and possibly losing her heart was enough to scare the boots off her.

Jake dipped his paintbrush into a coffee tin filled with turpentine to clean it. He thought about Marni and still couldn't believe what had happened. She had willingly come into his arms.

If Kate hadn't come home when she did . . . it had taken him a while to cool off after she had retreated to the barn.

Jake finished cleaning the brush and put it away. Then he took the turpentine jug and poured some of the oily liquid onto an old rag. He worked at the paint on his hands, contemplating them. Marni's actions today proved to him she'd soon be his.

He frowned. She *wasn't* his. He didn't even *want* a relationship.

Did he?

Even if he did, he could barely keep Marni still long enough to kiss her, and when he did she bolted like a scared horse. His actions had been really stupid, but he was at his wits' end. How could he get her to see him as more than a friend and still have her trust him?

Jake put away the rest of his materials, went outside, and got into his truck. He hadn't seen Marni leave her house and assumed she was hiding. He sighed. His truck rumbled onto the highway and the radio sang on about the terrible consequences of falling in love.

Marni was the type of woman who made forever seem like one drop of water on a drought-ravaged field. It could never be enough. She was the first woman to affect him like this, and as much as he wanted to blame this feeling on unrequited lust, he knew it ran deeper than that.

When his stomach started to rumble, he pulled into Mavis's Diner for a bite to eat. Love might feed the weary soul, but it did nothing for the tired body. He found an unoccupied stool at the counter by the wall and settled himself on it.

"What's eatin' away at your insides, Sugar?" Sally peered at him over her order pad.

Jake had been to the diner almost every night since he started to work for Ben. Sally was always his waitress. She'd given up on flirting with him and now treated him like the rest of her regular customers. It turned out Sally was the resident waitress, bartender, and pop-psychologist of Mavis's Diner.

"Aside from my stomach, I can't say much."

"I've seen hunger make cowboys do some mighty strange things before, but I've never seen it cause a hangdog expression like yours on a man's face." She pointed her pencil at him. "That look is reserved for the unlucky in love. Queen of Hearts got you down, Sugar?"

"Well, I wouldn't exactly say that." Jake eyed the waitress dubiously. Maybe Sally would have some insight into his problem.

"It's that Marni gal, ain't it." Sally snapped her gum. "She's been in here some since the first time you two showed up together. Seems to me she's had the same expression on her face lately."

"Then why am I chasing her instead of kissing her?" Jake slapped a hand over his mouth. His question had come out more bluntly than he had intended.

Sally smiled and leaned down to rest her arms on the counter, bringing herself eye level with Jake. "It's *because* you're chasing her, Sugar."

He let his hand slide down his face until it supported his chin. "I don't understand. I'm not doing anything different from what I've done before."

"That's the whole problem. If I'm right, the women you've dated before want to be roped and tamed, if you'll excuse the expression. They're looking for a quick tumble in the hay with a cowboy who's man enough to fulfill all their fantasies. Marni's the type of woman you strive to keep forever."

"I didn't say anything about forever."

"You didn't have to. It's written right here." Sally bounced the end of her pencil off Jake's nose. "And here." She then pressed the eraser to his chest over his heart. "Now all I have to do is teach you how to catch a girl like Marni."

Jake looked down the long counter at the customers sitting there. The ones closest to him seemed to be absorbed in the conversation. One guy actually tipped his hat and gave him the thumbs-up sign. "Don't you have other people to wait on?" Jake asked.

Sally waved her pencil like she was swatting at a fly. "Gloria can handle them, this is more important."

Jake glanced back down the line. The guy who had given him the thumbs up was grinning and smiling. *That's just great.* His stomach growled loudly. Knowing Sally wouldn't feed him until he listened to what she had to say, he urged her on, "Okay, so what do I have to do?"

"It's simple, really. Just back off and give her some space."

"Won't she think I'm not interested?"

Sally patted his arm. "She might, but she'll wonder why."

"I still don't get it."

"Let me explain it this way, Cowboy. When you're trying to catch a loose horse in a corral, do you chase it around until you're both out of breath, or do walk in and let the horse get curious enough to come to you?"

"I let the horse come to me."

"Right. And he comes to you because you've given him the time to trust you and decide you're not a threat. The same thing applies to Marni. Stay in her sight, but don't hit on her. If she's really interested she'll finally get close enough to find out what you're up to. Then all you have to do is snap the lead rope on her and haul her to the church." Sally tapped the pencil on his nose again and stood upright. "So what can I get you to eat?"

Jake just sat there staring at her. Churches, lead ropes, and runaway horses wearing wedding veils raced through his head.

Sally smiled indulgently and turned back to the kitchen to holler at the short order cook. "That'll be one cow on a bun with a side of fries and a rancher's coffee—strong and black!" She returned her attention to Jake. "Don't worry, Sugar. You'll get it."

On the ride home Jake thought about what Sally had said. It made sense, really. Marni needed some time to adjust to what was going to happen between them. And it *was* going to happen he swore vehemently. So even though he'd be hard-pressed to do it, he would keep his hands and lips off her until she was ready. The next move would have to be hers.

The way back passed quickly and soon he was pulling into the drive of his ranch, the Lazy Lariat. This place had been his home since he was born. He had played cops and robbers with his brother and sister in the main barn. He had stolen his first kiss on the front porch swing.

When Jake left home for college and the real world, he thought he wouldn't miss the ranch. But the place kept a part of him and he didn't get it back until he returned home to take over the business. Losing the ranch now would be like losing a piece of his soul.

Jake made his way into the cool interior of the house. He peeled off his shirt and left it in the mudroom so he wouldn't track paint through the other rooms. His jeans were relatively clean and the few paint spots on them had dried so he left them on. His boots and socks came off next and he left them in a pile by his shirt.

All his thoughts about Marni had to be put aside until he took care of one more thing. He went into his office and picked up the phone, then sat in his padded leather chair and leaned back. He crossed his ankles on the desk and put the phone in his lap while he dialed.

"Hello?" A man's voice said on the other end on the line.

"Marco Graciani, please."

"Marco here."

"Hi. It's Jake Harrison."

"Oh, Jake. I was wondering when you were going to call. Ready to sell me some horses?"

"Yes, Sir. That's why I called. I'll have a couple at the Steer Horn Rodeo next Sunday and I was hoping you would come out to see them. After the rodeo I'll take you to my ranch to show you this years' crop of foals."

"Sounds like a plan to me, Son. I'll see you then."

Jake said goodbye and hung up. He needed this sale so he could prove he was making a profit. If the bank continued to think he was a high risk they would foreclose on him. Marco was his one shot at saving the ranch.

There was no way he would let his childhood home be sold to the highest bidder. He owed it to himself and to his family to do everything he could to save it.

Chapter Seven

Jake came by on Sunday to help Ben finish painting the fence. Marni thought he looked like chocolate cheesecake on a bad diet day as he stood on her front porch. Except being hungry for the cowboy would be worse than blowing any diet.

"I convinced Trish to switch your entries with Twister over to Chance for the Steer Horn Rodeo next Sunday."

"You what?" That only gave her a week to finish training the mare. "I don't think we'll be ready."

"You already are," Jake insisted. He leaned his long frame against the doorjamb. "I saw you working with Chance today. Besides, if you don't jump in now you'll waste the whole season. You've already put in two weeks of training on her."

"I don't know. . . ." Marni worried her lower lip. She noticed Jake's eyes were drawn to the action, but she didn't stop.

"So you two don't win the first time out," he continued,

looking away from her mouth. "The competition will show you where you need to sharpen up."

Marni considered what he was saying. He had a lot of faith in her and her ability to train Chance, and she hoped it wasn't unfounded. Still, what he said made sense. Chance was a quick learner and it was time for a test. "Okay. We'll go."

"Good." Jake nodded. "And Marni?" A grin stole across his face.

"Yes?" She braced herself. He was going to say something about the kiss. Something to embarrass her or make her angry, she just knew it. She'd hardly seen him since Wednesday and neither of them had mentioned what had happened.

"You'll do fine," Jake said before stepping off her porch and disappearing around the corner.

Marni returned to her kitchen where she'd been making herself lunch. She stood and stared at the refrigerator door. *He didn't do it*, she thought. There was no comment about the kiss, or anything.

She sat at her table and chewed on her thumbnail while she thought. Had he lost interest already? Were her kisses so awful the thought of repeating the experience repulsed him?

More likely he was mad at her. He probably thought she was a tease. He didn't know her emotions were in a constant whirl around him. She wanted him. She wanted to kill him.

Besides, he didn't *seem* mad. He seemed nice. Real nice. Not like he was trying to hide his true feelings. He seemed sincere.

That brought her back to her first thought. He wasn't

interested any longer. But that didn't make sense either. He'd been interested when they were together on Wednesday.

It occurred to Marni that Jake might be up to something. But for the life of her she couldn't figure out what it might be. He'd probably found someone else. An easier target like Carol-Anne or Sally. It was for the best, she assured herself. Her arrangement with Jake would run a lot smoother if it wasn't wrapped in emotional ties.

The opportunity to buy Chance was what really mattered to her. If she had to choose between the two, she was sure that the mare was the bigger prize. After all, a horse like her was one in a million. Cowboys were at least a dime a dozen.

She refused to be disappointed if Jake had found someone to replace her so quickly.

A knock at the door signaled another visitor. Marni looked up to find Kate breezing into her home. "I made some cold tea for the boys. Care to help me bring it out to them?"

"Sure."

"I've got some cups in my kitchen. I've already filled them with ice. If you could go get them," Kate directed, "I'll meet you at the fence."

Marni followed Kate out, then ran to the main house. By the time she got out to the fence both men were ribbing her friend. "I've got the glasses." She held up her offering. They both reached for a cup. Marni thought Jake was very careful not to touch her when he took his.

After the first trip, the women took turns going out to deliver refreshments. On her second outing back to the main house Marni became convinced Jake was purposely avoiding her. He kept his back turned and only acknowledged her with a "thanks" when Ben thanked her for the jug of cold tea.

It has to be a woman, she thought as she entered the cool interior of Kate's home.

When it was Kate's turn to bring out something to drink, Marni decided to test her theory. She spied out the window as Kate laughed and joked with the guys. Jake didn't avoid her because she was a safe married woman. No competition for his girlfriend. *Damn.*

What am I doing? Marni pulled her head back and dropped the edge of the curtain she was clutching. *So what if Jake has a girlfriend? He's allowed.*

Who is it? Carol-Anne? Sally? Someone new? "It doesn't matter who it is," she admonished herself. She walked into the kitchen to get a glass of water.

Marni had no claim on the man. He was free to do as he wanted. So why did she want him to want her? This was Jake. An arrogant, aggravating, pushy *cowboy.*

But she couldn't stop thinking about him. About his touch, the taste of him, how his lips felt pressed against hers.

Marni took a long swallow of water. Thoughts of Jake's kisses were not helping her distance herself from him. The problem was, every time she tried to stop thinking about him the images came faster and in more vivid detail.

She groaned in frustration and slammed her glass on the counter. Cold water sloshed over her hand. It cooled her skin but didn't do a thing for her overheated imagination.

"Something bothering you?" Kate raised her eyebrows as she walked through the kitchen doorway carrying her tray.

"Nothing," Marni blurted out. She moved out of the way and Kate set down her load on the counter.

"Nothing doesn't make you spill water all over yourself."

"I—" Marni didn't want to tell her it was about Jake. She needed time to sort out her jumbled feelings first. "I forgot to do something for work tomorrow."

"Another bank emergency?" Kate asked dryly.

"Yes." Marni backed out of the kitchen. "*Huge* emergency. It could cause a banking disaster in Okida." She scooted out of the house before Kate could corner her.

Coward, she thought as she walked across the driveway to her house.

When Jake got up the following Sunday he whistled through his morning routine and sang in the shower. He had to stop dancing long enough to shave, and then he was two-stepping his way out to the barn to load Bart into the horse trailer.

Ned, his ranch foreman, saw him and mumbled something about whiskey in the coffee.

Jake didn't care. His plan to nab Marni was working, he was sure of it; she had seemed pretty determined to get him to notice her when he was painting the fence with Ben last Sunday. He also thought he saw her peeking out of the curtains in the main house when he was talking to Kate. And hadn't she left several messages on his machine to confirm the rodeo for today?

Jake made a point of returning Marni's messages when she was at work and avoiding the farm all week. Now he was on his way to pick her up for the rodeo. They would go early to give Chance some time to adjust to the new setting. Kate and Ben would leave later since the rodeo didn't start until two o'clock.

"This is going to work," he told Bart as he loaded him into the horse trailer. "I've finally found a way to get under

Marni's skin." The thought made him start whistling all over again.

He knew Marni was as attracted to him as he was to her. The way she had looked at him the day they shared their kiss by the fence proved it. She was a hungry wildcat and he was dinner.

Jake got into his truck and shifted uncomfortably in his seat. He had to stop thinking about Marni that way if Sally's plan was going to work. No longer would he be the rogue cowboy claiming his woman. It would take a supreme effort for Jake to keep himself away from Marni, but he had to do it. From now on it was hands off.

Jake pulled into Ben and Kate's driveway at ten o'clock. He didn't have to look for Marni; she was at the barn door waiting for him.

"Hey, Good-looking," he said as he swung down out of his truck.

"Hi," she replied shyly. "How are you? I haven't seen you in a while."

"Oh, I've been busy," he said evasively. "You know what it's like. Besides, Ben's home this week so he really doesn't need my help."

"Of course." Marni turned quickly toward the barn and nearly ran into the door. "I was just asking," she babbled on, a red blush creeping up the back of her neck. "Being polite. Making conversation. Filling the silence. You know . . . talking." She looked over her shoulder at him, her jaw snapping shut so hard that he could hear the click.

"Any way you want to fill the silence is okay by me, Darlin'." Jake let Marni absorb his comment. If she didn't come around soon she would do some permanent damage to herself. *And that would be a shame.* Still, her nervousness was cuter than usual since she was trying to act like nothing was bothering her.

She turned an even brighter shade of red than before. She swung back to Chance and snapped a lead rope on before unsnapping the crossties. The mare snorted and balked at her abrupt movements.

If she's this skittish after a kiss, I wonder how she'll be if we . . . don't even go there, Harrison, or we'll never leave this barn.

"Ready?" she croaked, then cleared her throat. "I *mean*, are you ready to go?"

"How about I load Chance?" Jake took the rope. Marni's nervousness was making the mare dance in place and he didn't want to have any trouble loading her. "You can put your equipment in the back of the truck."

"Equipment. Right. Equipment would be good." Marni darted for the tack room.

Jake shook his head as he watched her retreat. "Makes you wonder what she's thinking, doesn't it?" he asked the horse beside him.

Chance nosed at his pockets, looking for something good to eat. When she didn't find anything she flicked her ears back at him, then forward again.

"I suppose your stomach is much more important to you than mine or Marni's problems, right?"

Chance nodded at him like she understood every word he said.

"What am I doing?" Marni stared blankly at the wall of equipment in the tack room.

She didn't know why she was being so jumpy around Jake. He had a girlfriend, for goodness sake! She was sure of it. It wasn't like he was going to attack her and kiss her senseless.

The thoughts *like last week* and *I wish he would* skittered through her mind. A feeling of regret stole over her as she recalled the kiss, knowing it would be the last one Jake was ever going to give her.

She played back every tantalizing detail. Even her desire couldn't compete with the frustration raging through her mind. If she was right about Jake, then he was strictly off limits. She could only have the memory of that kiss.

Marni put Chance's bridle over her shoulder and grabbed her saddle off its rack. She walked outside into the bright sunlight. What did it matter if Jake was unavailable anyway? He was a cowboy. A happily single cowboy with no intention of ever settling down.

He was the wrong kind of man for her. Even though Roy had hurt her, she still wanted to get married. She longed for a small farm with white fences and a few kids playing in the sunshine.

"What's got you down in the mouth?" Jake took the saddle from her and swung it into the bed of his pickup.

"Nothing much. Just thinking." She forced herself to relax.

"Is this all the equipment?" Jake placed his hand at the small of her back and urged her toward the truck.

So much for relaxed, she thought as her muscles stiffened. Her nerve endings throbbed all the way up her spine. "Yes." She stepped away from his hand, her mouth dry. This was going to be a long day.

The rodeo was near Wichita Falls. Marni wasn't too excited over the thought of being in the close quarters of Jake's truck for the next hour. Well . . . she was excited, but for all the wrong reasons. She'd have to work on tamping down her attraction to him.

Marni looked over at Jake's lean form. One long leg shifted to the gas pedal and they accelerated onto the highway. *It must be the urge to want what I can't have*, she reasoned. *You could have had him*, she reminded herself.

Of course, that was before *the* kiss. The kiss that felt so good she forgot his name, her name, and all the letters in the alphabet.

She squirmed in her seat and looked out the window. The view did nothing to distract her now. *Even Roy didn't have the ability to make me so—*

"What are you thinking?" Jake asked.

"—hot." *Oh God, did I say that out loud?* Marni looked over at Jake. He glanced at her with one eyebrow raised and a question in his eyes. *Yup, he heard me.* "It's really hot today." She tried to cover up her blunder.

"Uh-huh." He reached for the vent dial. "Do you want me to turn up the air?"

Marni shook her head. "It's not the truck that's hot, it's me." Her jaw dropped open as she realized what she had said.

Her reaction was nothing compared to Jake's. He slowed down the truck and horse trailer and pulled over on the side of the road. After his vehicle was parked, he turned and gaped at her. "What!"

Marni's mind raced. *What do I say? What do I say?* "I'm still hot from being outside." True, it'd been half an hour since she got in the truck and Jake had the air turned up so high she was just short of shivering, but she hoped he would believe her story.

Then she shivered. Darn it!

"You don't look hot." Jake unclipped her seat belt.

"Maybe I should check." He reached for her, snagged her belt, and pulled her across the seat. He put a hand to her forehead. "Cool as a glass of ice-cold lemonade."

Marni blushed as she caught his meaning, but before she could react he released her and started the truck and trailer back along the highway. He kept both his hands on the wheel and stared straight ahead at the road.

Yes, Marni thought. *It's definitely a girlfriend.*

That was close. Jake had been ready to pull Marni into his lap and kiss her straight into tomorrow. She hadn't looked like she would object, with her lips parted and her tongue moistening them.

Only his comment about the lemonade had saved him. When Marni blushed at his suggestiveness, he remembered he was supposed to play it cool and let *her* come to *him.*

It was hard to ignore Marni. There were so many things he loved about her. *Loved? Hold it, no one said anything about love.* He *liked* her. That was it. He would *like* to spend some time with her. He did *not* love her.

Yet Sally seemed to think differently. Jake could not ignore the fact he'd always fallen for women who had wanted something *from him* more than they wanted *him.* He was not about to love another woman who would throw him away when she was done with him. Marni may be the marrying kind, but Jake was pretty sure she'd never see him that way. Besides, she had the perfect reason to use him and he was the person who had given it to her. She needed a horse right now and he had one she could use. She might even use her womanly charms as a form of gratitude, but he didn't want her gratitude.

He wanted *her.*

He glanced over at Marni. She was looking out the window again. The sunshine made her chestnut curls glow and she reminded him of an angel. He knew then he would take whatever piece of heaven Marni was willing to offer.

Jake was surprised by his conclusion. He would accept Marni on her terms. It gave him something to think about for the rest of the drive.

When they got to the rodeo only a few competitors and the organizers were present. Jake parked close to the arena and they unloaded the horses. Chance snorted and looked around but seemed to accept her new surroundings as just another place to forage food from. Her eyes lit up when she saw the king-sized hay bag tied to the side of the trailer.

"I think Chance is going to like going to rodeos," Marni said as the mare dug hungrily into her food.

"That, or she'll develop a strange fondness for the horse trailer."

They worked quietly together to get their horses ready. They rode side by side around the rodeo grounds, and when Marni took Chance off on her own the little mare didn't seem to mind at all.

What a gem, Jake thought, but he wasn't sure whether he meant the horse or the rider. He watched Marni work circles with Chance, putting her through her paces at each gait. In two short weeks the pair had become a team. Jake could see the bond between horse and rider. Chance trusted Marni without question. He wished Marni would have the same faith in him.

As he watched the two work, it occurred to him there was something special he could do for Marni. He knew she didn't have the money to buy a horse right now, but he vowed to hold onto Chance until she could afford her. Even if it meant years.

Jake smiled. Having a reason to spend years at Marni's

side didn't seem like such a bad idea. There were so many things they could do to pass the time. His grin got wider and threatened to swallow his face.

When both horses were sufficiently warmed up Marni and Jake untacked them and left them tied up at the horse trailer. The parking area around the truck began to fill up quickly as the rodeo start approached. Jake scanned the various pickup trucks, SUVs and cars for Marco Graciani.

"Who are you looking for?" Marni asked.

She stood so close to Jake that their shoulders rubbed. A tingling sensation traveled through his arm. Like every time he touched her, the experience was electric. If he didn't already know it was the fantastic chemistry between them causing the effect he'd be wondering if Marni had a problem with static electricity.

"I'm looking for a man who's come to see you ride my horse," Jake answered. He looked down at Marni's surprised face. He liked doing that to her. Keeping her off balance so she never knew what to expect from him.

"He wants to buy some horses from me so he came today to see what Chance and Bart can do," Jake continued. She looked concerned, so he decided to let her in on his plan. "Don't worry, I'm not going to sell Chance. After the rodeo Marco will go back with me to the ranch. If all goes well, he'll pick out the horses he wants to buy then."

Jake considered adding the fact that the sale would save his ranch, but he didn't want to bog Marni down with his problems. No sense scaring her off with the fact he might have nothing to offer her at all. If he didn't have Chance there would be no reason for her to stick around, and he wasn't ready to lose her yet.

Jake spotted Marco making his way toward them through the crowd. He'd only seen the man once, but his appearance hadn't changed. Marco had a black handlebar mustache with a full head of silver hair. His sports coat, which Jake assumed he always wore regardless of the heat, and his gold belt buckle accentuated his heavy stature. Bowed legs made him look like he was constantly stepping around something when he walked.

"Afternoon, Harrison," the man's voice boomed over the crowd and made a nearby horse shy away from him. "Who's this fine-looking filly?" he asked with no less volume after shaking Jake's hand.

"Martina Lewis, Sir," Marni answered.

"Marco Graciani." The man's hand swallowed Marni's smaller one as he pumped it vigorously up and down. "Pleased to meet you."

"Likewise." She pulled her hand from his grip.

"Marni will be riding one of my horses in the barrel race today," Jake supplied.

"Great!" Marco enthused. "Great!" A few people turned to see what all the commotion was about.

Marni nestled in a little closer to Jake's side. *Probably protecting her other arm from another hand pumping*, he thought. He couldn't blame her for her reaction. He had the impulse to duck and run for cover every time the man opened his mouth. He hoped Marco would be as enthusiastic when it came time to buy some horses.

"Why don't you two kids run along and do what you have to do before the rodeo starts." Marco turned to leave, then rumbled over his shoulder, "I'll just sit quietly in the stands and watch the show."

Jake doubted the man could do anything quietly.

After he left Marni spoke up from Jake's side. "I hope he's not that loud around the horses when he's working with them. The poor things are liable to go deaf." She shook her head as if she was trying to clear out a blockage. "I know I am."

Jake laughed, but he secretly hoped Marco had someone else do the shipping for him. Those foals would bolt clear through the other side of the trailer with that man's loud voice booming behind them.

When it was time for Marni's run, Jake watched by the fence rail. He had knots in his stomach, but tried to put them down to common concern for Marni. He really wasn't *that* worried. He felt ill when they called her name and told himself it was the hot dog he had eaten for lunch. By the time she burst into the arena he finally had to admit it was anticipation twisting his insides apart.

The pair took the first barrel with ease and Jake released the breath he'd been holding. It's not that he thought Marni would fall again, but if she was thinking about her last run it could affect her and Chance's performance. The rest of her run went quickly and smoothly.

When Jake met Marni back at the trailer she just about threw herself into his arms. "Did you see us?" she cried. "Chance rode like a dream out there!"

"Not bad for your first time out," Jake teased.

"Not bad?" Marni put her hands on her hips and mock-frowned. "She was wonderful. You have to sell her to me."

"I will. I promise you, Marni. No one else will own Chance." Jake indulged himself and gave her a brief hug. When he stepped back he noticed her grin, but he was sure it was from what he'd just said about the horse and for no other reason.

It was a good day at the rodeo for everyone. Jake finished an impressive second with Bart in his roping class and Kate was gloating because she finally beat Marni in a barrel race. She confided in Jake she had to be smug now, because in a few more rodeos Chance and Marni would be beating the pants off of all the competition.

Jake had to agree. There wasn't a horse person out there who couldn't see what a great team the two made.

At the end of the day, Ben took Chance and Marni home with him and Kate. Marco followed Jake to his ranch. He waited in his car until Bart was unloaded and turned out in the pasture, then he met Jake at the barn door. They walked inside and Jake flipped on the light switch. His foreman had put the sale horses in the barn so they would be ready to show to Marco.

Jake gave a rundown on each of the foals. He listed their pedigrees, registrations, feeding programs, and the training done on them. He took Marco into the back pastures and showed him his stallion and broodmares. The tour ended in Jake's office with one man seated on each side of the heavy oak desk.

"So, Son," Marco boomed. "Guess it's time to talk numbers."

"That's what we're here for, Mr. Graciani." Jake leaned back in his chair so he wouldn't appear too eager. There was no sense in giving the man an edge.

"What kind of deal are you willing to give me on that Chance mare?" Marco's voice made the metal filing cabinets rattle.

Jake sat up straight, then relaxed his pose and clasped his hands on the desk in front of him. "She's not for sale."

"Seems to me every horse has its price. I could get a good dollar for her." Marco continued talking as if Jake hadn't said anything at all. He probably thought Jake was using some bargaining tactic.

Jake had to make the man understand he wouldn't sell

the mare under any circumstances. "She belongs to Marni. I can't sell her."

"What kind of game are you trying to play here, Son?" The man's voice got even louder than before and Jake winced. "You said at the rodeo that the mare was yours."

"She is, but I'm keeping her for Marni."

"Then she's not sold, which means she must have a price."

Jake was getting frustrated with Marco. "I'm sorry I can't sell her. But as you saw in the barn, I have a full brother to Chance you can buy. He's every bit as smart and quick."

"I don't think you understand, Son." Marco narrowed his eyes and his voice got dangerously low. "I want *that* horse." He leaned back in his chair and studied his fingernails. "You see, I've done my homework on you, Harrison. I know how badly you need this sale. It'd be a shame if I pulled out, wouldn't it?"

Jake knew not to fall for a line like that. All horse traders knew of a "better" deal somewhere else. "Then I guess I'll have to find another person to buy them. Someone who won't steal Marni's horse from her."

"Worse things can happen to a horse than getting stolen. Seems like the best ones are always the first to get hurt or dead. Breaks your heart to sell a favorite, but it's easier than watching 'em die in a barn fire or having to make the decision to put 'em down, ya know?" He leveled a stare at Jake. "Hate for your sweet little girlfriend to have to go through something like that." He stood up and straightened his sports coat. "Ever see a barn fire, Son?"

"No."

He shook his head. "All animals scream when they're frightened. Doesn't matter if they're horses, rabbits, or humans. But the worse is the silence that comes after the screaming stops. It's enough to give a man nightmares." He smiled. "I can find my own way out. You think about what I said."

Jake stared at the vacant doorway after the man left. At first he was stunned. He was sure Marco had just threatened him, Marni, and the horse. But surprise quickly turned into anger. "Something stinks in Texas and it ain't the cow patties." He picked up the phone receiver and dialed.

"Sheriff's Department. How may I help you?" a woman's voice asked.

"Sonny Reid, please."

"One moment, sir."

Jake brooded about calling Sonny into this. It galled him to ask for the sheriff's help, but he needed to understand whether Marco was a threat to Marni.

"Sheriff Reid, here."

"Sonny, it's Jake."

"Harrison? What do you want?"

Jake explained how Marco had tried to convince him to sell Chance and their ensuing conversation about accidents and barn fires.

"What do you want me to do about it? Call the SPCA? The guy hasn't done anything."

"Could you look into the records and see if you have anything on Marco Graciani?"

There was a pause at the other end of the line. "Sure," Sonny finally said. "But if I don't find anything you're going to owe me big time."

Chapter Eight

J ake tried to forget about Marco while Sonny worked on the problem. He had said it could take a while since he had a heavy caseload at the moment. Instead of worrying over what he couldn't do anything about, Jake followed the rodeo circuit with Marni.

At the Bulls 'N' Broncs Rodeo, Marni and Chance placed third. At the Wildcat Rodeo they placed fourth, then two weeks later at the Circle Star Rodeo, they won the barrel race. Jake knew the two would do well together, but he was surprised at how well. Marni told him Chance was quickly surpassing Twister's best times in the same pens.

Jake had a lot of people ask him about Chance. The answer was always the same, she wasn't for sale. She belonged to Marni. Every time he said it, his heart gave a little hitch and he mentally added, *like me.*

Ben and Kate asked him over for dinner to celebrate Marni's victories. She was quickly closing in on her championship buckle and was currently tied for fourth place in the overall standings.

"Come on in." The door swung open before Jake had a chance to knock on it. Ben stood smiling on the other side.

Jake tugged his boots off and left his cowboy hat hanging on a coat peg. He followed Ben down the hall into the living room. Kate and Marni sat on one of the sofas with their heads tilted together in conversation.

"Hey, aren't the women supposed to be in the kitchen cooking?" he kidded.

"Nope." Kate smiled at her husband. "Ben lost the coin toss. It's his turn to cook tonight."

"Ben's cooking?" Jake turned as if to leave the room. "No one said Ben would be cooking. I think I have a sick horse to check on at home."

"Sit down," Ben growled, "or else you can join me in the kitchen."

Jake plopped down on one of the chairs and chuckled. He stretched his legs out in front of him. "Trust me, you don't want me cooking. The food I make tastes so bad, even the dog won't eat it. I'm lucky if I can whip up a pot of coffee."

"S'okay, Jake." Ben leaned against the doorframe. "You can always set the table, do the dishes, polish the silver—" A timer went off in the kitchen. "Looks like you've been saved by the bell." He left to check on the meal.

"So, what's the *chef* cooking tonight?" Jake asked. "Please tell me it's not peanut-butter-and-jelly sandwiches."

Kate laughed. "Believe it or not, Ben actually can cook. We're having pot roast with glazed carrots and home-baked biscuits."

"Wow!" Jake sat up. "Any chance you two are getting divorced so I can marry him? He could work on the ranch all day, cook for me at night, and I wouldn't have to pay him."

"No way, Cowboy," Ben said from behind him. "You eat too much and you don't shave your legs." He walked back out the door headed toward the dining room. "Supper's on."

They followed Ben out of the room. The round table was already set with steaming plates of food. Jake sat down beside Marni. "Are you down from cloud nine yet?"

"No, never. Chance is great. Thanks for letting me work with her."

"Thanks for training my horse. I wouldn't have had the time." He smiled at her and she smiled shyly back.

"If you two are finished," Ben interrupted, "supper's getting cold."

"Leave them alone, Honey." Kate put her hand over her husband's. "You remember what it's like."

Marni made a funny squeak-like noise, and when Jake looked at her she was turning red. She obviously knew what Kate was talking about, but he was in the dark.

"Remember what *what's* like?" Ben asked.

Kate looked at Marni and Jake. "When you're falling in love," she stated matter-of-factly before digging into her meal.

Marni's squeak turned into a squawk. She appeared to be trying to say something, but no words came out of her open mouth. Jake felt the same way. He was glad he hadn't been drinking anything, because he didn't want to repeat the episode at the diner. His tongue and elbow ached just thinking about it.

Ben looked back and forth between the two of them. "You two are in love? How come no one told me?"

"No!" Marni blurted out.

"Why would you think we're in love?" Jake asked.

Ben shrugged and looked at Kate.

"Good pot roast, Honey," was all she said. When everyone continued to stare at her, she added, "Aren't you going
to eat? It's getting cold."

They ate in silence after that. Jake supposed the food
tasted good, but if it had tasted like sawdust he wouldn't
have noticed. Kate's comment had hit him like a mule kick.
Why would she think they were falling in love? Had Marni
said something? Was she falling in love with him?

No way. Kate had to be imagining it. Putting a romantic
spin on things. But as long as he knew her, Kate had never
once been prone to a fanciful notion. Ben was more of a
romantic than his wife.

Jake glanced over at Marni. She seemed to be having as
much trouble eating as he was. She sat straight as a fence
post beside him. Her movements were stiff and she was
trying to avoid touching him. He wished he could read her
thoughts. If he only knew how she really felt. . . .

*You do know how she feels. She hates cowboys, remem-
ber? And you, Harrison are a bonafide pure-as-one-
hundred-proof-whiskey-genuine-COWBOY.* The thought sat
in his stomach as heavily as Ben's pot roast.

Marni raised her head and looked at him. She blushed
as their eyes met, then shrugged her shoulders as if to say,
'How was I to know?' The color in her cheeks and the
sparkle in her eyes made her look beautiful, like a woman
who was loved.

Jake smiled and winked at her. He kept that little piece
of information to himself. Kate could play matchmaker to
her heart's content. If he was right for Marni then he would
find out in time. No amount of pushing on Kate's part
would make things happen.

After dinner they all headed back into the living room.
Jake was going to sit beside Marni, but after a warning

glance from her and a look over his shoulder to see Kate watching them from the doorway, he chose a chair instead. He didn't want to encourage this awkward situation.

As they all settled in their seats, Ben cleared his throat. "Now that we have you two buttered up there's a favor Kate and I would like to ask of you."

"Shoot," Jake said.

"Sure, whatever you want," Marni added.

"Well . . . as you know, Katie and I are celebrating our fifteenth wedding anniversary this year. I never got to take her on a proper honeymoon because we were young and in love, not young and rich. So this year I'm taking her on a cruise."

"Sounds great," Marni said. "When do you leave?"

"How does this Friday sound?" Kate asked.

"But that's tomorrow!" Jake exclaimed.

"We would have told you sooner, but Ben wasn't sure he could get the time off work and I only got the tickets confirmed yesterday."

"It's okay," Marni assured them. "You know I can take care of the place on a moment's notice."

"And I'll help her," Jake added.

"It's not necessary." Marni turned toward him. "I can do it."

"I know you can," he argued. "But I can help. You have to go to work early in the morning and it only makes sense for me to come in and do the barn chores."

"I could get up extra early."

"Why would you want to when I can do the morning feeding?"

"Because I don't need your help. I can handle it. I'm sure there are other things you need to take care of at your own place."

Jake was pretty sure she was being quarrelsome to prove a point. She didn't want Kate to continue thinking they were an item. But darn it, she didn't have to be so prickly. He only wanted to help her. He frowned and tried to think of a better argument, but Ben interrupted them.

"If you two are finished," he looked at each of them in turn, "we'd like *both* of you to help us out around here. I have some projects for Jake to work on, and while he's here he might as well do the morning chores."

Kate spoke up. "Marni, you can feed the horses after you get home from work, and if you have time you can check on things in the house for me."

Jake looked at Marni. He felt like he was a little kid again, arguing with one of his sisters. Except Ben and Kate weren't his parents and he didn't feel very brotherly toward Marni at all. "Fine with me." He raised an eyebrow at Marni. "Any objections?"

She slid down a little in her seat before directing her answer to Ben and Kate. "No," she said softly. "That will work for me."

"Good." Kate stood up. "I don't mean to rush you two out, but we have to leave early tomorrow and I haven't finished packing yet."

"You won't have to worry about taking care of the place," Ben grumbled. "Kate will have packed the whole farm in her suitcase by the time we leave. If you two don't watch it, you might end up in there too."

Jake got up and stretched. "Mmmm . . . a vacation on a cruise ship. I could use some R&R. Babes in bikinis can do great things to heal a man's tired soul." He glanced over at Marni and smiled evilly before adding, "What color's your suit?"

She scooted out into the hallway without answering him.

He admired the sway of her hips as she walked toward the door. *Life's too short not to notice the little things that make you happy . . .*

Kate cleared her throat beside him. Apparently she had noticed him noticing Marni. He shrugged and winked at her before pulling on his boots. No sense in trying to deny the obvious.

Kate wished them good night at the door and left them standing alone on the front porch.

"Walk you home?" Jake asked.

"I don't think that's necessary. I only live across the driveway."

"I insist. A rampaging stampede of wild horses could come barreling out from behind the barn and trample you. It'd be much easier to perform a rescue if I was already at your side."

"Don't you think we'd hear them first? A herd of horses makes a lot of noise."

"Of course we'd hear them. But you'd be paralyzed with fear and I'd have to carry you to safety."

"I don't think anywhere is safe around you," she murmured before she stepped off the porch.

Jake caught up to her in a couple of strides and soon they were standing in front of her door. He wanted to kiss her good night and ached to hold her, but she still appeared to be nervous around him, especially after Kate's "love" comment.

He touched her cheek. "Sleep tight, Marni." She raised her lips toward his, but he kissed her forehead instead. "See you tomorrow." He could feel her eyes on him as he walked toward his truck. It took all his strength not to go back, sweep her into his arms, and say good night properly.

* * *

As soon as Kate and Ben left for their cruise, Marni grew apprehensive about the thought of spending so much time alone with Jake. The more time she spent time with him the more she had to admit she wanted something to happen between them. Thursday, when he'd kissed her good night, she had expected it to be on her lips, not her forehead. She'd gone to bed feeling restless and unfulfilled.

Jake wasn't around on the weekend. He had told Marni he would be working on his ranch to clear his schedule. The solitude Marni usually valued felt lonely with everyone gone. More than once she caught herself picking up the phone to call Jake, but she hung up before he answered, knowing she had no reason to bother him.

Marni didn't see him again until Tuesday night when she got home from work. He greeted her at her car after she pulled to a stop.

"Hi," she said, getting out. "How did things go today?"

Jake looked over his shoulder at the barn. "Well . . . everyone is still standing," he said slowly.

She felt a moment of panic before she realized he was kidding her. She smiled at him. "I'll just get changed, then I'll be out to feed the horses."

"I already fed them their dinner. I stuck around to let you know so you didn't feed them twice."

"They would have liked that. Thanks for telling me. Can I offer you dinner since the horses don't need me?"

"That's all right, Marni. I have plans."

Jake looked in a hurry to leave and she couldn't help feeling disappointed. "Oh." *Rats! It must be a date.*

He hesitated in his departure. "It's my mom's birthday," he explained. "I wanted to get home to call her and see if she got the flowers I sent."

"Oh!" Marni felt like a heel. Here she was feeling sorry

for herself because she assumed Jake had a date, and he was in a hurry to get home to call his mother. "I don't want to keep you. I hope she has a great birthday."

"Thanks." Jake started to leave again and then turned back. "Are you okay? There isn't something wrong, is there?"

"No, no, I'm fine!" Marni answered cheerfully. "I just expected to have more to do when I got home and now I don't know what to do with all my free time." It sounded lame, but it was the only excuse she had.

"If you're bored, you can come home with me. I'll cook."

Yes! "No way. Your cooking will kill me. I'll be safer if I make my own dinner."

Jake laughed and waved good-bye as he got in his pickup truck. "See you later, then." He pulled away and left her alone.

Marni immediately felt his absence. Dinner with him would have been fun. *What are you thinking? Dinner would have been a disaster. And how would you keep your hands off of him when he suggested dessert?*

She thought about that. She wasn't so sure she *wanted* to keep her hands off Jake anymore. He was sexy, sweet, and proving harder to resist than homemade chocolate fudge. The girlfriend thing was an obstacle, but she wasn't positive he had one. He had never mentioned someone else.

And, she thought as she walked into her house, *he rushed home to talk to his mom, not off to some hot date.*

Still, he hadn't kissed her on the lips when he said good night on Thursday. Marni had thought he'd wanted to, but something had seemed to hold him back. She really didn't know what was going on with him and she wouldn't unless she asked him.

I can do this. I'm an attractive, self-confident, strong woman, not a mouse.

I'm a spineless jellyfish, Marni thought as she rolled out of bed on Saturday morning. She had avoided Jake all week because the thought of actually asking him if he was involved with someone else sent her senses reeling. Now it was the weekend and her chances of seeing him were nil because he knew she wasn't working and that she'd be able to take care of the chores herself.

Marni pulled on her clothes and headed into the barn. She switched on the radio before she walked into the feed room. She loaded up buckets of feed and turned to leave, almost spraying their contents all over the floor when she saw Jake leaning against the doorframe.

"Morning," he said, then smiled. He came into the room and took the buckets from her. "I already fed the pasture horses before you came out."

"Thanks." Marni let him leave the room first so she could admire the way his lean backside flexed in his snug-fitting jeans. "I didn't expect to see you here today." She struggled to raise her eyes above waist level.

"I thought I'd help you feed the other horses, then take you out to breakfast. Since I didn't stay for dinner the other night, I wanted to make it up to you."

"You don't have to make anything up to me. You had something important to do."

Jake turned from the horse he was feeding and locked eyes with her. "I *want* to take you out. I can't think of any other way I'd rather start the morning than sitting across from a beautiful woman at breakfast." He glanced over his shoulder at her and winked.

A flush crept up her cheeks. At least he was finally showing some interest. She grabbed a wheelbarrow and rolled it out to the hay barn so she could think about what she should do next. Jake followed her out. *For a guy who's been scarce lately, he's sure sticking close now.*

Jake climbed to the top of the haystack to throw some bales down for her. The way he stood at the top of the pile, with his eyes glittering and a smile teasing his lips, he looked like a boy playing King of the Castle.

"You know," he drawled, "there's room for two up here." He wiggled his eyebrows.

"I think the horses will get fed faster if I just stay down here." He had no idea how hard it was for her to do just that.

"I had to try." Jake shrugged. He tossed down some bales, then half-climbed, half-slid down the haystack. He took the loaded wheelbarrow from her before she could roll it into the barn.

Jake and Marni fed the horses quickly and left them quietly munching their hay. They drove out to Mavis's Diner and found it was full when they pulled in. Luckily there was an empty booth in the corner.

Snap. Snap. Sally's pink bubblegum cracked in her mouth. "Morning, y'all. Coffee?" She held up a scratched pot and two mugs. At their nods she put the cups down and started pouring. "Haven't seen you two in a while. What have you been up to?" One blond curl bounced off Sally's nose when she looked up at them. She swatted it away.

"We've been busy," Jake said.

Sally glanced at each of them and nodded slowly. "I'm *sure* you have." She grinned and winked at Jake. "A man like you could keep a girl *real* busy."

Marni cleared her throat. "Actually, I've been busy at work." She picked at a crack on the table.

"There's been a lot of banking emergencies in Okida lately," Jake added.

Marni kicked him and he jumped. Her aim was a lot better than Kate's.

"Oh," Sally said. "I've known lame horses who move faster than you two. Get on with it already." Without waiting for a response to her comment she continued, "What can I get you to eat?"

After their orders were placed, Sally left the table. "Did you understand what she was talking about?" Marni asked.

Jake stretched his arms across the back of the bench seat and his legs across the floor. His boots brushed hers. "Sally seems to think we're headed to the hitching post together."

"Huh?"

"You know, marriage, happily ever after, wedded bliss."

Attempting to sip her coffee, Marni inhaled a large gulp and scalded her mouth. She winced in pain.

"Jeez, if I knew you found me so repulsive I never would have mentioned it." He looked at her seriously. "Are you okay?"

She nodded. "You surprised me and I burnt my tongue."

Jake leaned forward and whispered, "Want me to kiss it better?"

"I'mallrightreally." Her words rushed together.

"I don't know," he teased. "It sounds like you might have done some permanent damage. It could need medical attention and luckily I know first aid." He paused and smiled before adding, "I'm especially good at mouth-to-mouth."

Marni was saved by the return of Sally. Jake looked at Marni in a way that did funny things to her insides. Made her feel reckless.

She tried to concentrate on eating her breakfast, but her eyes drifted back to him. When he caught her, she held his gaze for a moment, then looked down at her food. It became a game of stealing glances to see who would get caught. She hardly tasted her meal, she was so busy devouring Jake with her eyes.

The ride back to the farm was in silence. Tension as thick as a spring fog spread out between them. Marni wondered what to do next. Should she unfasten her seat belt and slide over next to him? Maybe put a hand on his knee? She wanted Jake to understand she was attracted to him. She wanted to kiss him again.

"Are you staying to work?" she asked as they rolled down the driveway.

"I've finished all the projects Ben left for me." He stopped in front of the barn.

Marni was disappointed. Jake was going home and her flirting hadn't worked. It must have been too subtle. "Thanks for breakfast. I guess I'll see you later."

"Who said I was leaving?"

He got out of the truck and Marni jumped down from her side. The afternoon heat blasted her with its intensity. It was nothing compared to the fire burning within her. She felt like she would crumble into cinders because of the cowboy she desired so deeply.

"I thought you might have something to do at your ranch," she said. "You've been gone all week."

"Everything there seems to be running smoothly." He came around to her side of the truck. "I've been catching up in the evenings, but my foreman and the boys really don't need me there all the time." He closed in on her and she could smell his cologne. "So, now that you have me all to yourself, what do you plan to do with me?"

What is a girl to do with a one-hundred-percent sexy-as-sin cowboy? she asked herself.

Jake watched for Marni's response as he reached over the side of his truck into the bed. She seemed to be thinking about her answer, but she didn't run. He thought she would bolt for sure when he pulled out his roping gear. Her eyes got impossibly round as she eyed his equipment.

He knew what she was thinking and gave her his best smile before backing off. The plan was to seduce her, not scare her away again. "Ever done any roping?" he asked.

"Roping?" Marni seemed puzzled. "I used to when I was a kid," she recovered. "Haven't done much lately."

Jake pulled another rope from the truck bed. "Feel like practicing with me? I think I saw a roping dummy in the tack room."

"Sure. I have nothing better to do."

"I'm so glad I could be your last resort," Jake said dryly.

"I didn't mean it *that* way." She glanced at him. "Oh, never mind. . . . I'll go get a bale of hay, you get the roping dummy."

Soon they had the plastic calf's head stuck into a hay bale out behind the barn, close to one of the freshly painted fences. A few tosses of her rope and Marni was back in good form.

In more ways than one, Jake thought as he admired her lush curves. Rope coiled at her hip, wrist swinging her lariat. A slight flush rose up her neck from her blouse where it lay open at the collar. Her eyes sparkled as she eyed her target and he wondered if it was from the company as much as from the exercise. She looked like the cowgirl of his dreams. And she was.

"You're pretty good with a rope," he commented, swiping his brow of sweat caused by the stiff Texas heat.

Marni released her loop and snagged the calf's head yet again. "Thanks, my mom taught me." She smiled and looked off into the distance toward the pastures, lost in her own thoughts. "She used to call me her little cowgirl. Said I could have it all if I just set my heart on it."

"Where's she now?"

"She died when I was seventeen. Never even got to see me graduate from high school. I wish she could be here now and see how close I am to the championship."

"Is she the reason you want the buckle so bad?"

Marni nodded. "It was her dream for me, but it was mine too. We would train the horses together and I would ride them on the high school rodeo circuit. I miss the teamwork. She wanted me to be just like her.

"After she died my dad seemed so lost. He's obsessed with the idea his time on earth is coming to an end. He wants me to win a championship before he dies so he can take the message to my mom that I grew up to be just like her."

"Don't you think you already *are* like her?"

"Yeah." Marni smiled. "I guess I am."

"Do you have any other family?" Jake probed. He didn't want her to think he was prying, but he wanted know more about her.

"I have three older brothers."

"Now I know why you're so tough with me."

She smiled at him. "Yup. I had to learn how to hold my own at a young age. They were no end of torment to me. Now they're all spread out, I hardly get to see them."

Jake turned toward the hay bale and threw his loop, snagging the dummy easily. Dust rose up from his boots as he moved to retrieve his rope. "I think I'm glad your brothers live far from here."

"Why is that?" Marni looked perplexed.

"Because by now they would have beaten me black-and-blue for almost everything I ever said to you." He winked at her.

Marni raised a single eyebrow at him. "If I wanted you beaten up, I could have done it myself. I gave all my brothers their fair share of bruises when I was a kid. Even broke Cole's nose once."

"Whoa!" Jake took a step back from Marni. "What made you do that?"

"Cole told one of my dates he'd be singing soprano if he so much as laid a hand on me. The poor guy was so scared he wouldn't even hold my hand. When I asked him if he'd like to go out again sometime, he shouted no and peeled out of the driveway."

"I take it your brother is a big guy?"

"All my brothers stand over six feet tall and were defensive linemen on their high school football team."

"And I thought *you* were intimidating."

"How about you?" she asked. "Do you have any siblings?"

"Yeah." Jake smiled as he thought of them. "We're all equally defective in the relationship department."

"What's that mean?"

"Well, aside from my parents, who are happily retired and living in married bliss on the coast, I'm pretty sure all Harrisons are doomed to fall for the wrong people. My sister, Abby, married then divorced some rich blue blood. After which she moved up to Kentucky and started her own racing and training facility. Tyler got left at the altar by his cowgirl, so he chose to pursue his doctorate over women and gave up everything country to be the medical officer on a cruise ship."

"And you?" Marni posed the question shyly, not even looking at him as she spoke.

"Let's just say things are looking up for me and leave it at that."

She glanced at him, her lips parted on a silent "oh".

"How about a game?" he suggested to ease the uncomfortable silence.

"A game? What kind of game?"

"A rope-off. Each of us stands twenty feet away from the dummy and throws their loop. Every time one of us misses, the other gets a point."

"Sounds easy enough."

"There's more." Jake smiled as the idea came to him. It was so simple he just had to get Marni to agree to it. He wanted her to let down her guard and trust him, but before she did she'd have to get know him better. Hopefully his game would let her do both. "Every time one of us loses a throw, he or she has to answer a question for the winner."

"Like truth or dare?"

"Yeah . . . make it truth-or-dare-roping, but the winner gets to chose whether the loser tells a truth or accepts a dare."

"Are you sure you want to bare your darkest secrets to me?"

He shivered dramatically. "It's a risk I'm willing to take if you are."

"I haven't done anything like this since I was a kid. I guess it could be fun. . . . Okay, lets do it."

He let her have the first throw, and despite her earlier nervousness she snagged the dummy without any trouble.

When it was his turn he caught the plastic calf's head as well. He retrieved his loop. "See, an even match."

Three throws later Jake missed. He'd been thinking about what he would ask Marni when he got the chance and lost control of his loop.

"I do believe you owe me a dark secret, Cowboy."

"What do you want to know?" Jake asked.

Marni clasped her chin between her thumb and fingers. She made a slow walk around him, eyeing him up and down. He could feel the burn of her gaze as she assessed him. "Hmmm," she mused as she stopped again in front of him. "Did you have a teddy bear when you were a kid?"

"Huh?" He frowned at her. "Not the question I was expecting."

Marni grinned at him. "Come on, Jake. Haven't you ever heard that showing your vulnerable side is sexy?"

"If that's what you really want to know." He shrugged. "I had a scruffy, blue, stuffed dog I used to drag with me everywhere. He finally fell apart when I was seven."

"Did you have a name for him?"

Nuh-uh, no way, he was not going to tell her what he called the dog. It was too embarrassing. "I already answered your question. You only get one for every throw I miss."

"If you say so, but get ready to answer because I'll be asking next chance I get."

"Don't you want to know about my family, or my ex-girlfriends, or my favorite scar?"

"Not anymore." Her smile was pure mischief. "The more you protest, the more I want to know what you're hiding."

"Then I just won't miss another throw." Needless to say he did.

Marni giggled at his distress. "It can't be that bad . . . just tell me."

"Oh, all right. . . ." He sighed. "I called him my *Wuggy Dog*. I don't know where the name came from, but there it is. Happy now?"

Her grin almost stretched past her ears. "You have no idea." She stepped up to take her throw. "I would have expected you to name him Spike, or Killer, but *Wuggy Dog* is so much better."

"Give me a break, I was three. I'm sure you had a favorite stuffed animal with a silly name."

"Nope." She released her loop and missed the dummy. "I grew up as one of the boys. I played with dinky cars more than dolls. I did have this one doll though. . . ." She turned to look at him. "Her name was Annabelle. I thought she was the most beautiful girl I had ever seen. I made up a story about her being a fairy princess trapped in a doll's body." She sighed. "I think my father might still have her in the attic."

Jake reached out to her and brushed his fingers down her cheek. "I think someone broke the spell and let the princess out."

She blushed, a red crimson slash that spread across her cheeks like the setting sun. "I'm hardly an Annabelle . . . more like a Raggedy Ann." She pulled away from his touch. "Truth or dare?"

"Truth, Marni. Why don't you believe me when I tell you you're beautiful?" He watched as a tumult of emotions passed through her eyes: confusion, pleasure, doubt.

"People pass out compliments like candy at Halloween. Rarely do they ever mean what they say."

"I mean it. In my eyes you get prettier every time I see you."

She smiled and shook her head. "I believe you, Jake, but beauty is a subjective thing. A pretty face doesn't mirror the true person."

"It certainly doesn't in your case."

"Hey! What's that supposed to mean?"

"It means I think what's contained in here," he laid a hand over his heart, "is more lovely than your physical body could ever reveal."

"Oh . . . thanks." She gave him a quick peck on the cheek. "Your throw."

Jake wasn't really interested in the game anymore. He wanted to hold Marni in his arms and not think about the past or the future, just enjoy the moment. He missed his next two throws. Marni asked him what his first kiss was like and what his most embarrassing moment was.

He didn't mind answering her questions. He was biding his time. She would miss sooner or later. He didn't have to wait long.

"Ask away, Cowboy. What skeleton do you want to see now? My first love? My worst date?"

"Nope. I get the feeling you'd answer those questions whether we were playing a game or not, so this time I choose dare."

"I don't like the look on your face, Jake. How awful is this going to be? It's not going to hurt is it?"

"I hope not." He smiled. This was going to be good. She'd never see it coming, especially from him.

"Enough with the suspense, just tell me so I can get it over with as fast as possible."

"I dare you. . . ." He drew out the words. "I dare you to fall in love with a cowboy, Marni. I dare you to fall in love with me."

Chapter Nine

Marni's heart thundered in her chest. Fall in love with Jake? Ridiculous. She had sworn to never love another cowboy. She wanted someone safe and sweet who would never leave her. Jake was spontaneous, goofy, and he could raise her temper in a flash. He'd had his sweet moments too. She still couldn't believe he'd loaned her a horse for the rodeo season when he barely knew her.

But love him?

"I don't know what to say. I—"

He pressed a finger against her lips. "I didn't ask you to say anything. I'm daring you to take a risk. You can't do that with words, you have to do it with actions." He coiled up his lariat. "I've had enough roping for one day. Why don't we saddle up a couple of the horses and go for a ride?"

"Um . . . sure . . . well . . . I don't know . . ."

He took her rope from her loose fingers. "It's just a ride, Marni, not a life-long commitment." He winked at her, then walked off to his truck and threw his gear in the bed.

"What about your girlfriend?"

"I don't have a girlfriend . . . yet." He turned back once he got to the barn door. "You coming?"

She hoped she didn't look as dumb as she felt. Her brain couldn't keep up with the information he was throwing at her.

She followed him into the barn and tacked up Chance. Once they were back out in the bright afternoon sunshine he held her horse for her while she mounted.

"I was thinking we could follow the bush line back to the creek bed on the edge of the property." He wiped a light sheen of sweat from his brow. "It should be cooler out there."

It was cooler once they reached the shade of the trees and Marni found herself relaxing. The ride was far more enjoyable than she would have expected, and the main reason was the company. Jake was charming and suave, telling her stories about his family and his childhood.

He made her laugh when he described an incident involving his first girlfriend, her big brother, and a pitchfork handle. Somewhere in the course of the afternoon she realized she'd fallen for him long before he'd asked her to. She might even love him a little bit, but for the time being she decided to keep the information to herself.

Marni spent the rest of the weekend getting to know Jake better. He took her out to dinner Saturday night, took her fishing on Sunday, and just generally spent as much time with her as he could. Life became normal on Monday. She went to work, and when she returned to the farm that evening she found that Kate and Ben had made it back earlier than expected. Jake had already welcomed them home and left. She was disappointed she had missed him.

The rest of the week dragged by, as she got to steal only

moments from him and one quick visit at his ranch. It was weaning time for his foals and it was necessary for him to spend more time on the farm. Marni missed having him around. She longed to hear his voice, his teasing, to taste his kisses.

Kate tried to pump Marni all week for information, but she avoided the questions. In time she would confide everything to her friend, but for now she just wanted to keep the memories close to her heart. Even a week later she still had a hard time believing Jake was hers. He had found his way into her heart and he hadn't destroyed it.

She suspected Kate had guessed something had happened, but refused to ask outright. Marni was glad for the privacy. She was sure she loved Jake, but when the time was right, she wanted him to know first. Needed him to know she trusted him.

Early Saturday morning Marni called her dad.

"Tumbleweed! How's my favorite daughter doing?"

"Oh, I'm fine." She actually felt great. It seemed like her life had finally turned around. "How are you?"

"Well, my knees have been giving me some trouble lately and my old ticker hasn't been so great either."

"What's wrong with your heart?"

"It's been giving me the slow burn every time I eat chili."

"Dad, how many time's have I told you to lay off the hot sauce?"

"Do you expect me to give up everything I love? I haven't got long to enjoy this life as it is."

"Well, I guess hot sauce won't kill you but at least keep some antacids handy."

"So how's your race for the championship going?"

"It's actually why I called. Since I'm so close to winning it, I was hoping I could convince you to come out to the rodeo finals and watch me."

"Well, Honey, you know I couldn't possibly travel so far."

"But *you're* the one who wanted me to win this championship so much." Marni twisted the phone cord in her fingers. She knew it wouldn't be easy to get her dad to leave the house, but she had to try. How else was he supposed to move on with his life? He had to get over her mother, and she hoped that seeing her win this championship would do it. "Dad, you can't lock yourself away and not feel anything. If you do, you're already dead."

"You know how I feel about this, Martina, and I'd appreciate it if you didn't argue with me. Now, tell me some more about this fellow who's loaned you a horse. You said he's a cowboy?"

Marni sighed. Her father had chosen to stop living and there wasn't much she could do about it. It was up to him to change his mind. "Yeah, he owns a ranch over in Meridian."

"I thought you didn't like cowboys and tried not to associate with them whenever possible. It seems to me you were afraid of finding another Roy."

"Jake's okay."

"Good to hear, Honey. It's nice to know someone's looking out for my girl."

A knock sounded at Marni's door and she checked her clock. It was time to leave. "I have to go, Dad. Kate's waiting for me. I'll talk to you soon. Love you."

"I love you too, Tumbleweed. You take care."

She hung up the phone and raced to the door. If they

didn't leave soon they'd be late. She would deal with her father later.

Marni, Ben, and Kate met Jake at the rodeo where they parked the two trailers side by side. There were more spectators around because the circuit was drawing to a close and this was one of the few rodeos left before the finals.

Marni noticed Carol-Anne was in fine form. She was all decked out in a sparkly western blouse with silver fringes to match the *Rodeo Queen* banner that hung over her shoulder and was pinned at her waist. A rhinestone tiara twinkled on her silver-bellied cowboy hat and her jeans were so tight Marni swore you could make out dimples.

Carol-Anne was fawning all over Jake as he made his way back to his truck, but for once Marni kept the old jealousy away. It was another sign of how much she trusted him. He looked at her as he weaved through the crowd and didn't even seem to notice the rodeo queen clinging to his arm. Marni smiled slyly at him and blew him a kiss before ducking behind the back of Kate and Ben's horse trailer.

Jake was by her side in seconds without Carol-Anne in sight. "What did you do with your friend?" Marni asked. She darted a look over his shoulder as he backed her against the trailer and sent shivers of anticipation racing down her spine.

"I told her I smelled money and sent her in search of Marco Graciani." Jake leaned down to kiss her.

"He's here?" Marni pulled away reluctantly. "Shouldn't you talk to him? I mean, you haven't made a deal with him yet, have you?"

A look of concern passed across Jake's face, but he covered it quickly. "I don't want to talk about it," he mumbled against her lips before he kissed her.

She knew something was odd about that, but any other questions were forgotten as Jake's touch washed them away. She was frustrated when he pulled away.

"We'll finish this later," he said, stepping back. "I promise." With a wink he was gone.

She distracted herself with Chance, getting her ready for their class. They were already qualified for the rodeo finals. In the point standings they were sitting a close second to the championship. The thought made her smile, and she had Jake to thank for all of it.

"Afternoon, Ms. Lewis," Marco said as he sidled up beside her. "Remember me?"

"Of course, Mr. Graciani," she answered brightly. "How are you?" She didn't particularly like the man but would make polite conversation for Jake's sake.

"Call me Marco, my dear." He paused to wipe the sweat from his brow. "I'm not doing so well, I'm afraid."

She was sure he'd feel better if he just took off his sports coat. "Really?" She continued to brush Chance.

"I can't seem to corner that boyfriend of yours. It's almost like he's dodging me on purpose. I really wanted to talk to him."

"He's avoiding you?" Very odd. "Why would he do that?"

"He may have his reasons, but I'd like to know whether he's settled on our deal or not. Otherwise there's no reason for me to stick around too long."

Marni had the distinct feeling that the man was talking about leaving in a larger sense than not staying to watch the rodeo. But it really wasn't any of her business. "If I see him I'll let him know you came by," she offered.

"Thank you, Ma'am." Marco gave Chance a solid pat on the rump that caused her to pin her ears back and snap her teeth at him. "Have a nice afternoon." With that he waddled away into the crowd.

The whole conversation felt very weird to Marni, but she didn't have time to dwell on it since her race was to begin soon and she had to warm Chance up. She looked for Jake in the exercise pen, then again before she entered the arena for her race. It was strange not to have him by her side, giving her a few last pointers before she ran.

When she took second place it really didn't mean anything until she returned to the horse trailer and saw Jake waiting there for her with a big grin. "You looked good out there, Honey." He helped her off her horse and gave her a resounding kiss. "That championship is going to be yours."

"Thanks." She pulled away from him and began untacking Chance. "Where have you been all afternoon?"

"Here and there, catching up with people." He smiled at her as she turned to look at him. "I knew your attention was focused elsewhere." He rubbed the mare's nose.

"Oh." *That made sense, didn't it?* Marni returned to what she had been doing.

"Don't tell me you missed me?" Jake took the saddle off the horse and returned it to the trailer.

"I wouldn't say that. It might cause your head to swell."

He grinned at her and her stomach did jumping jacks. "I promise I'll make it up to you tonight for being away so much this week. I'll make you dinner after the rodeo. Consider it a celebration. If Ben and Kate are ready to go now, then I'll meet you at your place after I drop Bart off at the ranch. Okay?"

"Sure. I forgot to tell you, Marco—"

"First call for the calf-roping class," a voice blasted over the loudspeaker, cutting her off. Marni was almost certain a look of relief crossed Jake's face when it happened. *What was going on?*

"That's my class, I have to go." He grabbed her shoulders and pulled her toward him. "But not before I get a kiss for good luck." After the quick peck he untied his horse, put on the bridle, and then hurried for the arena.

"I guess I can tell him about Marco tonight," she said to Chance as she brushed her down. "Maybe then he'll be settled down enough to explain what's been going on today."

Jake was relieved he could delay talking about Marco for a little while longer. He still hadn't heard from Sonny and he didn't want Marni worrying about his problems with the ranch. It had nothing to do with her, he reminded himself when a pang of guilt over his secrecy stabbed him.

As a result of thinking about Marni and the things he was keeping from her, Jake missed his calf when he worked his class and received a "no time". He returned to his trailer with Bart and brooded about his ride. He rarely missed a throw. He knew Marni was the reason. She had gotten under his skin, and if she so much as coughed he'd worry something was wrong.

Jake saw Marni and the others off before he went back to the horse trailer. They wanted to get back to take care of the rest of the farm chores. He hurried to untack Bart. He'd take his horse home, then go over to Marni's for dinner. The thought immediately improved his mood.

Sonny came around the side of the trailer on his horse. "Harrison," he barked. "We need to talk."

Jake looked up. "Now?"

"No, I'll come by your place after dinner. Say . . . seven o'clock?"

"All right." Jake wanted to put off the meeting. He really wanted to see Marni, but this was important too. It had to be information about Marco. "Come up to the house."

"Just make sure you're there. You've managed to get in the middle of something serious." Sonny tipped his hat and rode off into the sea of horse trailers and trucks.

Jake watched him disappear and his mood darkened. "Could this day get any worse?" he asked Bart.

Apparently it could.

On the way back to the ranch, his truck overheated and he had to wait for it to cool before continuing home. As it was, he didn't make it back to the Lazy Lariat until 6:30. He just had time to call Marni before Sonny arrived and tell her that he'd be late.

She picked up on the second ring. "Hello?"

"Marni, it's Jake." The tension in him began to unwind when he heard her voice.

"I thought something had happened," she said. "What took you so long?"

"My truck broke down on the way home and I had to wait for it to cool."

"Are you coming over now?"

Jake sighed. He *really* hated to let her down. "I'm going to be a little late; I have a visitor coming."

"Oh." She sounded disappointed. "A buyer?"

"It's about the horses," he answered evasively. "How about I call you when he's gone, and if it's not too late I'll still drop by."

"Sounds good." She seemed a bit brighter.

"I'll talk to you later, Honey." After she said good bye, he hung up, feeling somewhat hollow.

Minutes later Jake heard a vehicle coming down his driveway and walked out to his front porch to see Sonny's white truck rumbling toward him. At least the sheriff was prompt, and if he got rid of him fast enough he'd still have some time to spend with Marni. Besides, he hated to ask anyone for help, and the fact Sonny was the sheriff of Meridian made it even worse.

"Harrison," the man said as a form of greeting when he got out his truck. "Let's get to this."

Jake brought Sonny into the kitchen. "Can I get you something?"

"Sure. You wouldn't have a beer in there, would you?"

Jake took out two bottles, removed the caps, and set one on each side of his kitchen table. Both men sat down. Sonny took a long swallow before speaking.

"I've been looking into that Marco Graciani character you told me about. Turns out this is one of several aliases for a Cletus Jones."

"*Cletus?*" Jake took a sip of his beer, then chuckled. "So the slick *Italian Stallion* is actually a good ole boy?"

"I don't know about the good part," Sonny said. "The man's as slippery as a catfish in the mud. Turns out he's wanted on several warrants and has a rap sheet as long as my right arm. Insurance fraud is his primary scam."

"What does that have to do with me?"

"He's in the habit of scamming poor suckers like you out of their horses. Once he has what he wants he insures them heavily. There's always an accident of some sort. The horse ends up dead and Marco pockets the money.

"Last time he pulled this con, someone besides the horse ended up dead. It happened in Oklahoma. The sheriff's department there isn't positive whether Marco was directly involved in the guy's death, but they'd sure like to talk to him about it."

"Damn." Jake leaned forward. "What are you going to do?"

"You mean what are *we* going to do," Sonny said seriously. "If I'm going to catch this guy I'll need your help. When I talked to the other sheriff departments that have leads on him, they all said the same thing. The guy's as sly as a fox and he can smell a setup a mile away. We have to make this believable."

"What do you need from me?"

"Have you had any contact with Marco since we last talked?"

Jake found that when Sonny went into sheriff's mode he was easier to take—almost bearable. "I haven't, but Marni spoke with him today."

Sonny raised an eyebrow. "Any idea what was said?"

"No, but I haven't told her what's been going on. No one, other than you, knows my suspicions."

"Good. The less people who know the better. What I can't figure out is why he chose you as a target: you're a rotten calf-roper."

"It's not me he wants, it's Marni's horse, Chance. Besides, you know I have good horses. Even your dad wants them for breeding."

"But why would Marco go after *your* stock when there has to be an easier victim around?"

"He told me he did his research and he knows that I'm losing my ranch."

"You're losing the Lazy Lariat?" Sonny looked genuinely concerned.

"I think I'm going to have to sell it before the bank does it for me."

"I had no idea. What happened?"

"Dad let things get run down before he retired. It took

all my savings and a second mortgage to get the operation running again. And then, of course, there was Carol-Anne. I haven't recovered my expenses yet. Marco was supposed to be the big spender who saved my butt."

"Where would you go if you sold the ranch?"

"Back to the city. I have a standing job offer in Dallas. I could pick up where I left off." Jake got them each another beer out of the fridge.

"But if you left there would be no one worth competing with on the rodeo circuit. Not to mention who would I insult?"

Sonny's comment gave Jake a pause. "You mean you *like* arguing with me?"

"I'm not saying I'd miss you when you're gone, but it keeps things interesting having you around." The sheriff stared at his beer and picked at the label on the bottle. "So why is it you always give *me* such a hard time, Harrison?"

"Keep it up and this is going to become one of those touchy-feely moments."

"Gimme a break." Sonny grinned.

"If you must know, I always thought you were the spoiled little rich kid. You had the best things money could buy and I had to work my tail off for every little thing. I guess I was jealous."

"I couldn't help it my parents had money, but that was when we were kids. You," Sonny pointed a finger at him, "still give me a hard time every chance you get."

"I'd hate to break a long-standing tradition," Jake kidded. "Besides, you give back as much as you take."

"You have no idea how hard it was to compete with you. I had the money, but your family had deep roots in this town. I was just a wanna-be cowboy next to you."

Jake thought about that. He'd never known it had been hard for Sonny. "Guess we were both wrong."

"Now who's turning this into a touchy-feely moment?" Sonny took another swig of his beer. "Don't go all sweet on me, Harrison. I still don't like you."

"And this isn't putting Marco behind bars either." Jake steered the conversation back to its original topic. "So what's your plan?"

"We need to lure him out into the open so I can arrest him."

"Like the rodeo?"

"Jeez, Cowboy, you're smarter than I gave you credit for," Sonny ribbed. "At the rodeo it'll be easier for my deputies to hide in the crowd."

A thought hit Jake. "Isn't he dangerous?"

"I'm not sure he killed that guy, but we'll have to be careful just the same. I wouldn't want innocent people getting hurt. 'Course if you get shot, I'll just consider it a necessary risk." The sheriff grinned at him.

"Thank you so much for your compassion, Sonny. How do we get him to the rodeo?"

"Since he wants your horse Chance so much we'll use her as bait. You call Marco and tell him that you'll sell her and you wanna make the exchange at the rodeo finals."

"What do I tell Marni?"

"You don't tell her anything other than you're selling your horse to Marco," Sonny said. "It's too big a risk for her to know anything more than that."

Jake felt a lead weight drop into the pit of his stomach. This wasn't going to be easy. He shifted uncomfortably in his chair. "But I promised to sell Chance to her. I can't disappoint her like that, even if it is just pretend."

"Your problem. She has to think this is real."

"And I don't doubt you'd love to comfort her when I let her down," Jake accused. "You'll ride in with your blazing silver star and white hat and make her an offer she can't refuse."

"You know what they say, Cowboy, *all's fair in love and war*." The sheriff tipped his hat and left the kitchen. However, the anxiety that gnawed at Jake's insides stayed. He dreaded the conversation he was going to have to have with Marni, so he decided to call Marco first.

Jake went into his office and stared at his phone. He tried to summon up the appropriate enthusiasm. When he was finally ready, he dialed.

"Graciani here."

"Marco, I'm ready to talk business."

"Glad to hear it, Harrison. Somebody finally talk some sense into you?"

"You might say so."

"If it's okay with you, I'll just take the mare first," Marco said. "I have an immediate buyer for her."

I'll just bet you do, Jake thought darkly. *A plastic bag, a horse trailer rigged to let go on the highway, or maybe a horrendous barn fire.* The images turned his stomach. "I thought maybe I could bring her to the rodeo finals and you could pick her up there, since I have to get her from Marni's place first anyhow."

"Sounds good to me, Son. I don't live too far from there."

"Good," Jake replied woodenly. "I'll see you Saturday."

"Don't let me down, Son. It'll hurt you more than me if you do." On that ominous note Marco hung up the phone.

Jake stared at the phone. He shook off his feeling of dread and thought about calling Marni. In the end he decided to postpone the confrontation with her until the next day. He called and apologized for not being able to make it. She didn't seem too happy with him, but accepted his excuse that he had a broken fence to repair. A real repair job would be nothing compared to the fences he'd have to mend with her when she found out he was going to sell her horse.

One day turned into two, and when Marni decided she couldn't take it anymore she went to track Jake down at his ranch. He wasn't avoiding her, she reasoned. Why would he be?

Of course, he could have called. No, she wouldn't let herself think that way. He was probably just too tired at night to call her. If something was wrong he'd tell her when he saw her. There was no sense worrying about him.

When she pulled down Jake's long driveway he came out and stood at the porch railing waiting for her to park. "Hey, Beautiful," he said as she got out of her car.

"Hey yourself, Cowboy." She was glad to see him. He looked so good. A well-worn pair of jeans hugged his thighs and a smile graced his lips. "I hadn't heard from you so I thought I'd just drop by after work. I hope you're not mad." She gripped her car door waiting for him to tell her to leave.

"Anytime you want to surprise me is okay by me." He came down the steps, closed her door for her, and swept her into his arms. "I missed you too," he said, then kissed her. Her lips tingled with the touch she'd been wanting for days. When he pulled back, she almost whimpered with desire.

Seriousness darkened his features and her stomach churned in anticipation of bad news. "What's wrong?" she asked.

Jake shook his head. "There's something we need to talk about, but let's go inside where it's cooler and I'll get us both something to drink." He walked up the porch steps and held the door open for her. "I'll meet you in the living room."

Marni preceded him through the door and into the dim interior of his home. She'd only been inside once before, but nothing had changed. The furnishings were few but enough to fill the rooms. In the living room a large fireplace covered with photographs decorated one wall.

As she reached for a picture, she heard Jake put glasses down on the coffee table. She didn't turn toward him until he stood beside her.

"They're my family." He pointed at the people in the photo. "That's my sister, my brother, and my mom and dad."

Jake and his sister shared their father's dark hair and blue eyes, but his brother's hair was blond and his eyes were green like their mother's. She stared at the picture of the family sitting together on the front porch steps until Jake took the frame and placed it back on the mantel. He ran a finger down her cheekbone and watched her like he was trying to memorize her features. When she opened her arms to him, he clutched her in a tight embrace and took her lips in a kiss that was passionate and almost seemed desperate.

Reluctantly, Marni stepped away from him. His intensity concerned her. "What is it you wanted to talk to me about?" He was acting like a condemned man being granted his last request.

Jake sighed deeply and walked over to the sofa to sit down. Marni followed and picked up one of the water glasses that were on the table. She wasn't thirsty but wrapped both hands around the cool surface to keep from reaching for the solemn cowboy who sat beside her. As much as she wanted to touch him, she also wanted to know what had him acting so strangely.

"There's someone interested in buying Chance," he stated.

The sick feeling returned to Marni's stomach in force. "You know I still want her. I don't have enough money yet, but in another month—"

Jake shook his head. "The man who wants her is very insistent and he's made an offer I can't afford to refuse, so I'm going to accept it."

"You're selling my horse!" Marni's rising panic made the question into a statement. She struggled for control over her emotions, but it was a battle she was doomed to lose.

"It's nothing personal," he continued, obviously ignoring the turmoil he was causing. "I have to protect my investments. Besides, there'll be other horses."

"Chance isn't just any horse, she's special. Please don't ask me to give her up."

Jake really looked at her then. He had to be able to see he was tearing her apart. When she thought he was going to change his mind his jaw tightened and his eyes hardened. "This is ranch business and I expect you to understand and trust I am making the right decision. I *have* to sell this horse."

The man she'd fallen in love with was breaching the promise he'd made to her. When Roy had betrayed her, she'd been left with broken dreams and a bleeding heart. This would be far worse because she loved Jake so much more.

"She's just a horse. I have lots of others you can choose from in the field."

Marni barely heard him over the roaring in her ears.

"How can you say that? You're breaking your word to me! Chance means everything!" It was more than that. Marni had believed him when he said he would only sell the mare to her. He was violating his promise and betraying her trust. Why had he given her his word when he didn't mean to keep it?

The glass of water she held trembled in her grasp. Jake removed it and set it on the coffee table. She wished she'd dumped it over his head when she had had the opportunity.

He tried to take her hands in his, but she swatted him away. "Is this the reason for the gentle kisses and tender looks?" she accused. "Were you trying to soften me up?"

A muscle jumped in his jaw and he got up and paced the room. "Do you even think past that horse? If I didn't know better . . ." He stopped and crossed his arms over his chest.

"What?" she blurted.

"I'm wondering if you're like the rest of the women I've been involved with. Using me to get your championship buckle like they would. The dumbest part is, I would have let you use Chance without the coy little games you spent so much time playing. My only question is, if you wanted to pay me back for Chance that badly, why not jump into bed with me? We could have been having fun so much sooner. After all, I was a sure thing from the beginning."

"How could you think I'd ever do that?" Marni's voice cracked. It was bad enough he was stealing her horse from her, but now he was accusing her of giving herself to him. "I can't believe—" She stood up abruptly and walked to the door.

"Marni, wait!" Jake followed her.

"If you want Chance that badly you can have her." She opened the door. "Just be sure you leave me alone."

"Wait!"

"I swear I'll never fall in love with another cowboy as long as I live!" She slammed the door behind her, bolted down the porch steps, and successfully kept the tears away until she got in her car.

Jake saw the hurt in her eyes, knew his words were cruel, but he couldn't stop them. Marni had become the focus of past pain from others who had claimed to love him. He despised himself, but it was the only way he could protect his heart from this amazing woman while she was breaking it into small pieces. When he realized he was wrong and that her feelings were true, it was too late. She'd already walked out his door.

He held the knob and leaned his head against the cool wood. All the energy left his body. He'd just made the worst mistake of his life. She'd never take him back.

"I love you too," he whispered into the empty room.

With a heavy heart, Jake returned to the living room and sat down. He'd like to blame their argument and subsequent break-up on Marco. But he knew that wasn't true. Marco wasn't the one who accused Marni of using him for one of his horses. That had been Jake's own stupidity.

He realized that in the heat of their argument he'd never asked Marni to bring Chance to the Mason Jar Rodeo finals. He got up and went to use the phone in his office. She wouldn't talk to him, so he'd leave a message on her machine.

After three rings her cheery voice answered and instructed him to leave his name, number, and a brief message. "Hi Marni, it's Jake. I'm sorry about the things I said, but I still have to sell the horse. Can you bring Chance to the rodeo finals on Saturday? You can have your barrel run and after that Marco will take her. I . . ." What did he want to say? He should tell her he was wrong, he loved her and was afraid of losing her. "I'll leave you alone if you do this for me."

Marni drove around for hours before returning home. When she got back she listened to the message on her machine. Jake had said he would leave her alone after the rodeo and her head told her it was for the best. However, in her heart she wished he'd ask for her forgiveness and tell her he loved her too. What hurt the most was realizing she had opened her whole heart to him and he hadn't trusted her at all.

"When will I learn?" Marni wondered aloud. "I deserve more respect than these cowboys can afford me. I deserve a better man." But she didn't *want* another man; she wanted Jake.

In time you'll get over him too, she assured herself. But she really wasn't so sure. Jake was different. *This* was different. She had thought she had been in love with Roy, but when she'd left him she hadn't shed many tears. All she wanted to do right now was curl into a ball and cry for days, then sleep until the pain went away. And that might take forever.

Sure, she'd been hurt when she caught Roy in the motel. She'd felt betrayed. It was nothing compared to the searing pain she felt when Jake had accused her of using him for Chance.

The phone rang shrilly and made Marni jump. She picked up. "Jake?"

"No, Tumbleweed. It's Dad."

Why did she think it was Jake? She didn't even want to

talk to him. Did she? "Hey, what's up?" She tried to sound cheerful.

"I have great news. I bought a ticket for the bus and I'm coming to see you win that championship of yours."

"Really?" This was the last thing she had expected. The last time she'd talked to her dad he'd been adamant about not coming. "But doesn't that mean you have to stay overnight?"

"It does, but I've decided you're right. There's no reason I can't leave the house for a couple of nights."

"Dad, that's great." And if she hadn't just had a huge argument with Jake she would have been excited. "Are you sure about this?"

"I'm sure this is the right time to see you. But I'm bringing my bottle of fifty-year-old scotch just in case."

"I'm so glad you're coming. I could use my dad right now."

"Why, Tumbleweed? Is something wrong with your horse?"

"Well Dad, Chance really isn't my horse." Marni figured it would be easier to explain this now than later.

"I'm not talking about her. How's *your* horse?"

"Twister's doing well. The swelling in his leg has gone down and he's putting some weight on it again. I should be able to ride him again next year." And that was the truth. No matter what happened to Chance, she still had a horse. All she needed now was her cowboy.

After she got off the phone, Marni busied herself in the kitchen making a meal she knew she wouldn't eat. Talking to her dad had cheered her up while it lasted, but once she hung up she felt sad and lonely all over again. As she worked she noticed the lights were still on at the main house and she wasn't surprised to find Kate knocking at her door a half-hour later.

"No pressure," she said, walking into the house. "I know you'll talk about it when you're ready. I brought Triple Chocolate Ecstasy," she held up an ice cream container, "and *Godzilla*." She held up the video and led the way into Marni's living room. "There's nothing like watching a hundred-foot lizard with PMS kick the hell out of New York to make you feel better."

She popped in the video and looked at Marni. "And if it doesn't . . ." She shrugged her shoulders. "Well, it's Ben's video and it's better then watching a romance. If we had *Terminator 2* I would have brought it over. What could be better than watching a woman on a rampage with heavy artillery?"

That brought a smile to Marni's lips. "How did you know I was upset?"

"Woman's intuition?" Kate ventured. "Okay, I confess. When you didn't come home from work, I called Jake to see if you were there. He told me what had happened. I'm really sorry, honey."

Marni shrugged her shoulders and tried to look like she meant it when she said, "It was bound to happen sooner or later. I know better than to put too much faith in these cowboys."

"You don't really mean that, do you?"

"No, but if you hug me and get all soft, I'm going to start blubbering all over you, and it's not going to be pretty."

"Okay, I'll stay back." Kate gave her an odd little smile and went into the living room to set up the VCR.

Marni got two spoons from the kitchen. They settled on the couch with the carton nestled between them. For a while she forgot how bad she felt as she watched the giant she-lizard trample New York. They cheered her on and booed at all the humans in general. Good or bad.

All too soon it was time for Kate to leave. She stood at the door clutching the video. "Are you sure you're going to be all right? I could stay if you want me to."

Marni nodded. "I have to be alone sometime. I might as well start now."

"If you change your mind you can come to the house. I'll kick Ben onto the couch and you can stay with me."

"Thanks." Marni hugged her. "I think I want to be alone right now."

"The offer stands," Kate said, pulling back. "Any time you need me." She gave her a small smile and walked off into the dark.

Later Marni roamed her empty house. She put away her cold dinner and got ready for bed. She turned out the lights, lay down, and did the one thing she rarely allowed herself to do. She cried herself to sleep.

Chapter Ten

Marni's stomach clenched as she looked at Chance. This was it. Today was the last ride she'd have with her horse and the last time she'd see her cowboy. Her anger at him had only cooled minutely over the days they'd been apart, but it didn't stop her from missing him. She just wished he'd been more honest with her from the beginning. Told her the horse would sell to the first available buyer. It wasn't fair.

Of course she had more than that to worry about. Today's finals were being held at the Mason Jar Fairgrounds in the same arena where Twister had fallen. Marni didn't think she'd have the courage to run in there again. To top it off, her dad was sitting in the grandstands right now, waiting to see her win a championship. She wasn't sure she could look at Chance without getting sick, much less ride her.

"Beautiful day for a rodeo, ain't it, Sugar?" Sonny ambled up to her, belt buckle gleaming and boots shining to within an inch of their lives. He looked like everything she had sworn off of. Twice.

"Every day at the rodeo is a great day," she responded automatically. She'd seen the same creed plastered across a dozen truck bumpers this morning alone.

"Only when I get to see your smiling face here." The sheriff winked at her.

"Huh?" Marni had begun to fast-forward through many different barrel racing scenarios, all of them ending with her and Chance in a mangled mess. Would Jake be there for her if she fell again? Or would he be looking after Chance, protecting his investment? She reluctantly dragged her attention back to Sonny. "I'm sorry. I wasn't paying attention."

"S'okay, Honey." He reached for her hand and started to knead it. "Everyone gets a case of performance jitters once in awhile, unless you're a pro like me."

"I . . ." She looked down at their linked fingers. "It's not exactly that."

He exhaled on a whistle. "You and Jake have a fight?" He tried to look sympathetic but failed.

"You might say that." Marni smiled, but it was a half-hearted gesture. It was hard to be cheery when her whole world was falling apart. She wanted to wrap herself in Jake's embrace and stay there until the hurt was gone. But he was the reason for the way she felt, so it wasn't possible.

"Did Jake do something? You don't have to be brave for me, Sugar, Sheriff Sonny's got big shoulders for you to cry on." He straightened said anatomy to emphasize them and puffed up his chest.

This time Marni's smile was genuine. She had to give the guy points for trying. It wasn't his fault she felt like she'd been stampeded by a herd of cattle. "I'll try to remember that."

He deflated a little when she didn't accept the offer to curl up in his arms and have a good cry. His thumb caressed the palm of her hand. "You know, we have a lot in common."

Marni itched to pull away, but she didn't want to be rude. There was no reason to be uncomfortable; Sonny was harmless. "Sure," she said. "We have a lot of the same interests."

He visibly brightened. "You bet, Gorgeous. We both like to rodeo *and* we both think Jake Harrison is a good-for-nothing-hound-dog." Sonny looked down at the toes of his shiny boots.

Marni winced. She knew what was coming next. He was going to ask her on a date and she'd have to turn him down. Jake was the only cowboy for her. *Last!* she corrected. *I mean, last.*

"Well, what I wanted to know . . ."

Please don't do it, please don't do it.

Sonny looked into her face. "Aw heck! You're in love with him, aren't you?"

She crumpled. So much for trying to hide it. "Yeah, I love the big fat jerk, but . . ."

". . . you had a fight," he finished for her.

She nodded. "We both said some pretty nasty things and now it's over. It's really for the best, I'm sure." But she wasn't sure at all. Jake made her feel alive. When they were together the world was vivid, filled with bright colors, crisp sounds, and strong emotions. Now she just felt gray.

"Do you want me to beat him up for you? Me and my deputies could do it."

"No, I don't think that's necessary." She smiled.

"How about I hold his arms while you beat him up? You'll have the law on your side. I'll declare it justifiable cause."

Marni giggled. "I don't think hitting Jake will make me feel any better."

Sonny pulled his hand away from hers. "Don't say I didn't offer. Maybe I'll punch him in the nose just to make *me* feel better."

"Sheriff!" she admonished. "You're supposed to uphold the law, not abuse it." A smile crept past her mock frown.

"Membership has its privileges, Baby." He gave her a peck on the cheek before leaving.

Marni sighed as she watched him go. His careless amble made her think of Jake. In the few days since their break up she'd found everything reminded her of him. Maybe she'd take a vacation far away, somewhere where she could forget about Jake, somewhere where there were no cowboys.

The parking lot was packed when Jake pulled in. The circuit was a small one, but it was important to the people who competed in it. The rodeo was also important to the communities that surrounded it. An influx of competitors and spectators supported the local merchants who had booths there.

After Jake parked, he worked his way through the crowd. By the grandstand he checked out what the vendors were selling. He needed a new cowboy hat, so he tried on some of the white straws while he waited for Sonny to find him at their designated meeting spot.

A tap on his shoulder brought him around and he saw the sheriff behind him. "Harrison," Sonny said. "Ready to catch us a criminal?"

"Absolutely," Jake growled, putting down the hat. Earlier in the week Sonny had explained the details of the plan. Marco would come to the rodeo to pick up the horse and sign the transfer of ownership papers. The sheriff and his deputies would be stationed close to the horse trailer. It was the easiest place to trap Marco since the lawmen could blend into the crowd. "Catch 'im, skin 'im, and hang 'im."

"Keep a tight rein on your attitude, Harrison," Sonny warned. "I don't want you scaring him off."

"Don't worry about me. I won't mess up your plans."

"Speaking of which . . . what are you going to do about the ranch?"

"Sell it," Jake answered bitterly. He'd thought all he really needed was the ranch, but he'd been wrong. He now knew he could live anywhere if Marni was by his side, but it wasn't meant to happen. "I have an appointment with the realtor this week."

"Cancel it."

"Why?" Jake shook his head in confusion.

Sonny looked like he was about to put something in his mouth that he knew he wouldn't like the taste of. "I talked to my dad last night. He's really happy with the mare you sold him. He wants to buy some more of your fillies to use as broodmares. The horses he races are getting hard to handle and he thinks a little cattle-horse blood will balance out the next generation. Are you interested?"

Jake was pretty sure he'd have to shovel his jaw off the ground and dust it off before answering. "Are you serious?" This offer could save his ranch. "How many horses are we talking about?"

Sonny's expression soured even more than it had at first. He crossed his arms over his chest. "How many will it take to keep you in Meridian?"

Jake was stunned. The sheriff couldn't have surprised him more if he had sucker-punched him in the gut. "Wh-why?" he sputtered out.

"I'm not doing this for you, you know. I'm doing it for Marni."

"But she doesn't want to have anything to do with me. Besides, if I'm gone you'd have a better chance with her."

"Don't think I haven't considered that. But *come on*, Harrison, you had a fight, she'll get over it."

"I don't know," Jake said skeptically. "I said some really awful things."

"Then she'll get over you and I'll have a shot."

Jake snorted.

"But if I have to see her pining over your sorry behind when you return to the city, I swear I'll track you down and shoot you myself."

"Darn it, Sonny, I never knew you cared."

"Like I care about a burr under my saddle blanket," the sheriff groused. "Now go find Marco before he gets suspicious and pulls another disappearing act."

Before he left, Jake blurted out one more question. "You're *sure* he isn't dangerous?"

"I already told you he isn't known to be. But then he usually slips away before anyone gets close enough to find out. Are you having second thoughts?"

"No! It's just that when I talked to Marco the last time . . . oh, never mind it's probably nothing."

"Tell me."

"I think he threatened me."

"What! What *exactly* did he say?"

"He said something to the effect of not selling my horse to him will hurt me more than it hurts him."

"Why didn't you tell me this before?" Sonny berated.

"This could change everything. If he really is a threat I would have never drawn him out into public like this."

"I had hoped it was an idle warning. Does this really affect your plan that much?"

"I'll let you know after we catch him." The crowd enveloped the lawman as he walked away.

His answer didn't make Jake feel any better. A voice behind him caught his attention before his thoughts became paranoid and he whirled around. "Kate?"

"Thank goodness I caught up with you," she said, slightly out of breath.

"What's up?" He was expecting to be chastised again for taking Marni's horse from her. But anything Kate called him couldn't be worse than the names he'd given himself over the past few days.

"I need your help." She grabbed his hand and hauled him into the crowd. "Now."

"What's going on?" Jake tried to keep up with her quick pace. This was the last thing he had expected. "Is there an emergency?"

She stopped abruptly and turned to face him. He crashed into her and had to grab her shoulders to keep them both from tumbling over. "Kate, what's going on?"

She looked up at him and he could see the concern shadowing her eyes. "It's Marni. She says she isn't going to ride. I've never seen her panic before. She won't even get on Chance to warm up."

"Why—" Realization hit him. "This is where Twister fell. Of course she's scared." And if she'd been feeling anything like he had she was already agitated before she even got to the rodeo.

Kate nodded. "Ben's trying to calm her down, but neither of us have been able to get her up on the horse. I know things aren't so good between you two right now and you're probably the last person she wants to see, but maybe . . ." She shrugged her shoulders.

"I'll talk to her. Where is she?"

"Out behind our trailer." Kate led the way.

When he saw Marni she had herself propped against the back of the horse trailer with her hands braced on her knees. She was shaking her head at something Ben had said. Her jaw was clenched and her face was white except for a sickly flush of pink across her cheeks.

Ben noticed Jake as he walked up. "Maybe you can get her on Chance. You know the horse better than I do." He tipped his hat and followed Kate away from the trailer.

"Marni," Jake said. "Look at me."

She raised her head and straightened. She balled her fists at her sides. He knew she was taking a stand against him as well as against riding. "I'm not going out there and you of *all* people can't make me."

Okay, so she's definitely still mad. "Why?" He wouldn't let her lose this race because she was mad at him.

"How can you ask why?" She paced the back of the trailer anxiously, her arms wrapped around her waist. "After what happened to Twister here . . ." She stopped and looked at him. "Chance is your horse. I'd think you would want to protect your investment."

Jake winced as she threw his own words back at him. So maybe this was about more than the horse. "If I thought you were in any danger at all I'd pull you off the horse myself."

"Well maybe *I* think I'm in danger." Marni glared up at him, but it didn't hide her anxiety.

He wanted to take her in his arms, kiss away her fears and her hurt, but she'd never let him do it, so he used words to soothe her instead. "I have full confidence in your ability to ride Chance. You're not going to fall."

"How do you know? The ground conditions haven't changed since Twister and I wiped out."

"Chance isn't Twister," Jake stated. "She's smaller and more compact. The shallow ground is easier for her to run on. She can sit down and slide around a barrel, whereas Twister needed to dig in. This is *her* pen."

Marni looked at him doubtfully.

He crossed his arms. "You know I'm right about this." Then he added for the benefit of both of them, "Trust Chance." The double meaning didn't go unnoticed by him. If he could just get Marni to take a chance on him . . .

She chewed on her bottom lip.

He hoped she could see how much he believed in her as she scrutinized him, then nodded.

"Okay," Marni said. "I'll do it."

Jake sighed with relief. "Good. Now go put her bridle on and warm her up."

"What's taking you two so long?" Kate charged over to the trailer. "Don't tell me she still won't run her class?"

Marni looked at Jake and nodded slightly, signaling she was ready to ride.

"She's running." Jake took the reins and put them over Chance's head, then he put his hands on Marni's hips and lifted her side-saddle onto the horse. She automatically swung her leg over the horn, her skin still tingling where he had touched her.

"Hurry up, Honey," Kate said. "They just started to drag the pen for the last cut and they're calling for you. You don't want to disappoint your dad."

"Your dad's here?" Jake asked.

"Yeah, he came all the way from Oklahoma to see me ride."

"Then what are you waiting for?"

Marni took up her reins and headed for the arena. She glanced over her shoulder at Jake and he waved at her and smiled. Would she really be able to give him up over a horse?

She got to the ringside and the chute boss scowled at her. "Didn't think you were ever going to get here," he groused.

"Me neither," she said under her breath.

She watched the other competitors complete their runs. Not a single one fell, not a horse slipped. Her stomach churned and she clenched her teeth. She and Chance were the last horse and rider pair to run.

Trust Chance. Jake's words echoed in her head. Marni scanned the grandstand and spotted Jake seated with Ben, Kate, and her dad near the second barrel. He believed in her. Was that enough?

She looked back toward the entrance and got the signal from the chute boss to enter the arena. With a deep breath, she sent her horse into a gallop.

She thought her heart would beat right out of her chest as they approached the first barrel. "Whoa!" she hollered and sat deep into her saddle. Chance slid around the can like a pro and it felt as though they were running on air.

Excitement bubbled inside Marni as they charged the second can. Clods of dirt and sprays of dust flew up from Chance's feet as she negotiated the turn. They shot out of that barrel and swooped toward the third one. This turn was as picture-perfect as the last two had been. Marni could barely contain herself as they ate up the ground to the finish line. The run felt good. Really good.

The enthusiastic whoop of the crowd confirmed it. "14.997!" the announcer shouted. "Folks, it seems we saved the best for last. Martina Lewis is our new champion!"

A swarm of people and horses surrounded Marni and Chance outside of the arena. The mare snorted and danced from the sudden attention. Congratulations came from the many voices around them.

A strong pair of arms circled Marni's waist and pulled her off the horse. When she turned to see who it was, Sonny gave her a quick hug. "You were great," he said sincerely. "You deserve the buckle. Especially since you had to put up with Harrison to get it." He winked and strode off.

Marni thanked all the people surrounding her and led Chance out of the crowd. She searched the grandstand, but it seemed Jake was already gone. At the horse trailer Kate and her father were excitedly waiting for her.

"Tumbleweed, I am so proud of you. It was worth the trip to Texas."

"Thanks, Dad."

"I think I'll be taking a lot more trips, too. I didn't realize how much I was missing until I saw you out there. I need to spend more time with my kids and live my life, not huddle away in my house and wait for death to claim me. Your mother never would have expected me to stop living for her sake."

"I'm so glad to hear that." Marni hugged him.

"Honey, I knew once we got you on that horse you'd be amazing." Kate enveloped Marni in a hug when she stepped away from her dad and Ben's large arms circled them both.

"Same goes." He smiled at her.

Marni looked past his shoulder. "Where's Jake?"

"He headed back to his truck with that Marco fellow,"

Ben answered, releasing the two women. "Said he had some business to take care of. He's really proud of you, though."

"Kate, do you think Trish will have the prize checks ready yet?"

"I don't know. It usually takes her a while to write them out."

"I have to get my check and stop Jake from selling my horse. Will you take care of Chance?"

"Absolutely!"

Marni tossed the reins at her friend and took off at a run. When she got to the entry booth, she launched herself into the swarm of competitors around it. "Trish, I need you! This is an emergency!"

The show secretary's head whipped up. "What is it, Honey?"

"Can I get my check now?"

"You know better than that. I still have to write out the checks for the saddle bronc riders."

"I wouldn't ask if it wasn't important."

"Tell me what's got your pants on fire and maybe I can make an exception for you."

"Jake's going to sell Chance, but if I can give him the money first I might be able to stop him."

"Good enough reason for me." Trish quickly calculated the prize amount and handed Marni the check. "I hope it's enough."

"It's going to have to be." She pushed her way back out of the crowd and ran to the parking lot. She *had* to find Jake.

A meaty hand grabbed Jake's shoulder and yanked him back before he could vault over the fence rail and congratulate Marni for winning her class.

"What's going on here, Son?" Marco bellowed over the cheers of the crowd.

"Good to see you too." Jake pasted a smile on his face. It was time to get this nasty business out of the way. Then maybe he could get Marni to take him back.

"I'd say the same if I understood why your little woman is riding my horse." He pushed people out of his way as he strutted toward the horse trailers.

Jake was taken aback by the man's abruptness. It seemed once he got what he wanted there was no need to be polite. "Chance isn't your horse yet. And I promised Marni she could ride the mare in the rodeo finals."

"We had a deal, Boy." Marco's gaze narrowed. "You're not trying to pull something on me, are you?"

Jake resisted the urge to roll his eyes. The con man was accusing *him* of funny business. "I'd think you'd be pleased. They won and now the horse is worth more to you."

"She would have been worth nothing with a broken leg."

You'd like me to think. "Seems like a moot point. The race has already been run."

Marco was still frowning.

"Why don't we go back to the truck and get Chance's registration and transfer papers. By the time everything is filled out and signed, Marni will be back with your horse."

Jake smoothed over the situation enough to get Marco away from the crowd and to the relative quiet of the parking lot. Now if he could only find the sheriff and his deputies. Did Sonny expect him to arrest the guy too?

When they got to Jake's truck he pulled Chance's registration papers out of the glove box along with a transfer of ownership form he needed to fill out. He rooted around in the compartment, stalling for time on the pretense of looking for a pen, until Marco handed him one over his shoulder.

"Try this one, Son."

The gold-plated pen dangled between the con man's fingers, looking as foreboding as a noose. Jake swallowed and wondered again where the sheriff and his deputies were. *I could be dead before Sonny pulls himself away from his herd of buckle bunnies.*

"What's the matter, Boy? Ain't never seen a pen before?"

"Of course." Jake grabbed it and started filling out the transfer form. He didn't want the con man to get suspicious.

"Wait!"

Jake turned and saw Marni running toward him.

"Don't you *dare* sell that horse!" She came to a stop in front of him and waved her prize check under his nose. "I've got the money for her right here."

"I've already made a deal with Marco. Why don't you run along and find a pretty pair of boots to spend your money on." He really didn't want to make her even madder at him, but if it got her away from the con man and the danger he posed, then it was worth it.

"I don't care! I'll double it."

"I think you better listen to your boyfriend and let the men take of business." Marco broke in.

"And since when is this *your* business?" Marni turned and punched a finger into the portly man's chest.

"Since I'm the man with the deal that's going to save your cowboy's neck."

"What's he talking about?" she asked Jake.

"Didn't he tell you the future of his ranch relies on this sale?"

Marni shook her head. She looked at Jake and he could

see her confusion. He just wanted to get her away from Marco before he did something. Sonny didn't know how dangerous this guy was. What if he had a gun? The need to get Marni to leave increased. "This doesn't concern you," he said coolly. He hoped the ice in his voice would force her away.

"The hell it doesn't! Why didn't you say something? You thought I wouldn't understand? That I would let you lose your ranch so I could have my horse? What kind of person do you think I am?"

He fought to control the smile that attempted to take over his lips. He admired her fire despite himself. First she was mad because he was going to sell her horse, now she was mad because he might lose his ranch because of the same horse. But it wasn't getting her away. He could offer her an explanation after Marco was arrested. "Marni—"

She cut off his statement with a slash of her hand and returned her attention to the other man. "Why is this sale so important?"

"The bank's breathing down his neck, Sugar," the con man drawled. "He needs to make some money soon or kiss his farm good bye."

"Why is it so important that you have Chance? Jake has lots of good horses."

"I already have a buyer for the mare, and frankly, if he doesn't sell her to me then the deal's off and I'll take my business elsewhere. So tell me, is that check of yours big enough to save your boyfriend's ranch?"

Marni shook her head and sighed, clearly defeated. "No, I can't afford to make him an offer like yours." She turned and faced Jake. "Maybe I shouldn't have pitched a fit over you selling my horse, but you should have told me about your ranch. I would have understood. I don't expect you to throw away everything you love for me."

"It took me a long time to realize that being a cowboy is a lonely life spent out on the range when you don't have a partner. And the ranch is just an empty house and a ramshackle old barn if you don't fill it with love," Jake said.

"Are you . . . are you trying to tell me you love me?"

"I—"

"This is sweet and all, but we have a business transaction in the works here," Marco growled. "Finish writing the *darn* transfer papers!"

Jake looked up and Marni let out a startled gasp as she turned around.

The con man had a gun pointed at them.

"Is that really necessary?" He managed to sound amazingly calm.

"I think it is. You two have a hard time keeping your priorities straight. Consider *this* incentive."

Jake squeezed Marni's shoulders to comfort her as well as himself.

"Now Ms. Lewis, I want you to go get me my horse while your boyfriend keeps me company. And before you think about running for help, remember I have a gun and I'm fully prepared to put an extra hole in him."

"Jake?"

"Just do what he says." He wanted to tell her to get Sonny, but there was no way he could without Marco overhearing.

Marni glanced back at him as she moved away. Fear radiated from her stiff posture. "Go," he said. "I'll be fine." She nodded, turning toward the horse trailers and walking swiftly away.

The con man aimed his gun at Jake. He couldn't wait

for Marni to return. He only had one chance. With a silent prayer he leaped at the weapon and attempted to wrestle it away from Marco. He managed to get the barrel pointed in another direction before it went off.

A resounding bang accompanied the wild shot. It ricocheted off a nearby horse trailer and then hit something out of sight. Jake heard Larry the blacksmith bellow and hoped the large man hadn't been hit.

"Jake!" Marni had returned. She was standing only fifty yards away from him.

"I'm okay," he grunted as Marco kicked him. "Get Sonny!" He could hear her running toward the grandstand.

"Give me the gun, Boy! Fighting isn't going to make me want to shoot you any less."

"Believe me, the feeling's mutual."

Another shot rang out. "What the hell was that?" they said in unison as three more retorts sounded. None of them were from the gun they were struggling with.

Jake used the distraction to rip the weapon from the con man's hands. As he did, it flew out of his fingers and rolled under his truck.

"Hold it!" Sonny roared from somewhere behind Jake. "Marco Graciani, get down on the ground and put your hands behind your head." This statement was followed by the distinct sound of a rifle being cocked.

"What took you so long?" Jake stepped back to let one of the deputies search the con man.

"You were supposed to be at the horse trailer, Genius. My deputies have been watching the mare, but we couldn't find you until the gun went off."

"Was anyone hurt?"

"Not yet. At least I don't think so, but you two started one hell of a ruckus. There's shots being fired all over the place." Another bang sounded, emphasizing Sonny's statement. "I swear, all of redneck hell has broken loose on the Mason Jar Fairgrounds."

"Sheriff! Sheriff! Earl Spenser just blew Bobby-Lee's Stetson clear off his head!" Virgil, Meridian's youngest deputy, came running into view waving his arms. "*And* Tater Banyon tried to shoot the saddle bronc judge. Tater chased him clear up into the grandstand before someone in the crowd wrestled his shotgun away."

"Then what are you doing here telling me about it?" Sonny pointed at the deputy cuffing Marco. "Take him to the squad car and keep an eye on him. Virgil, come with me and I'll show you how the law is supposed to handle a situation like this."

Marni came into view as the lawmen ran off in the direction of another shot.

"Jake." She threw herself into his arms. "Are you okay?"

"I am now."

"Good." She pushed him up against his truck and put her hands on her hips. "Then do you mind telling me what the *hell* is going on?"

Jake was more than happy to finally tell her the truth. "I was never going to sell Chance. It was a setup to catch Marco; he's wanted for insurance fraud and murder."

"Holy cow!" Marni punched his arm. "You could have been killed!"

"I'm *fine*"

"What about your ranch? Are you really going to lose it?"

"I was, but Sonny and his dad made me an offer that will save the place." He reached out to her and took one of her hands in his own. "I'm sorry about the secrets I had to keep from you and I'm really sorry I ever doubted the way you felt about me. Truce?" At her nod he leaned over and kissed her. "With everything settled at the ranch there's only one thing missing in my life . . ."

"Something's missing?"

"Yeah." He smiled at her. "I could really use a wife to help me fill that lonely house. A couple of kids would be nice too. So what do you say? Are you willing to hitch your horse at this cowboy's ranch?"

She stared at Jake dumbly. "Y-you w-want to—?" she stuttered.

"I'm asking you to marry me, Marni. I love you more than you could imagine, and all the other things in my life have no meaning if I can't share them with you." He paused. "I don't have an engagement ring for you, but maybe I can offer you Chance instead."

"Yes!" Marni threw herself into Jake's arms and kissed him. "Yes to you. Yes to Chance. Yes!"

Epilogue

The following spring

Marni sat at her kitchen table the night before her wedding, sipping coffee and swapping Jake stories with Kate and her soon to be sister-in-law, Abigail Blue.

"When he was five he tried to rope and hogtie the family dog." Abby's eyes sparkled with good humor. "After that incident Bandit hid under the front porch whenever someone pulled out a rope. Poor dog. He knocked over the ranch foreman and took out mom's flower garden running for cover one day."

A loud rap at the door interrupted the women's giggles. "I'll get it." Marni began to get out of her chair but was pushed firmly back down by Kate.

"No way, it's probably Jake again. Let Abby go. She can handle her brother better than I can."

"I couldn't handle him when he was still my *little* brother." She pushed away from the table. "But let me see if I can get rid of him."

183

From the kitchen they could hear Abby open the door. "Jake, go back to the main house. You can see her at the ceremony tomorrow. It's bad luck before then."

"You didn't believe in that goofy superstition when you got married."

"And now I'm divorced. See? Bad luck. Go away."

"Let me in, Sis. It's an emergency."

"Like the last two times?"

"This is for real, Abby. Chance got out of the barn and I need help catching her."

"Why not get Ben? Or better yet, I'll go with you."

"No, she doesn't know you. She won't come."

Hearing this, Marni shot out of the kitchen. "Just let me get my jacket. I'll be right out."

"Okay," Jake said. "I'm going to start looking for Chance." He turned and disappeared out the door into the night.

Moments later Marni followed him. "Are you sure you don't want Kate or me to go?" Abby asked.

"No. This shouldn't take too long anyway." She shut the door behind her and stood on the front porch, letting her eyes adjust to the dimness. "Jake!" she called when she didn't see him waiting for her.

She didn't get an answer, so she ventured off the porch into the yard. Figuring he was probably somewhere around the barn she set off in that direction. The full moon lit her path, saving her from stumbling along in the dark.

"Jake?"

"I found her!" His voice filled the quiet yard. "We're behind the barn."

Marni jogged to the back of the barn and saw him holding Chance. As she neared the two of them she noticed the mare's mane was braided with ribbons and daisies.

"She wasn't really loose, was she?"

"No." He placed the lead rope in Marni's hand. "But it was the only way I could steal you away from your bodyguards." His smile flashed in the moonlight.

"She's beautiful, Jake." She reached her free hand up and traced one of the flower petals.

"Not as beautiful as my bride." He lifted her chin, pulling her attention away from Chance. Lowering his head, he kissed her gently on the lips.

A soft sigh escaped Marni as he pulled away. "Why did you do this? Why did you *have* to see me tonight?"

"Because." Jake pulled her into his embrace. "Tomorrow is for our family and friends, but tonight is for us. I love you Marni, today, tomorrow, and always. And a church, some witnesses, and a fancy party aren't going to make you any less my wife than you are right now."

"I don't need those things either to know you're my husband. You're the cowboy of my heart and I love you."

"Always?"

She nodded. "And forever."